Praise for

CATHERINE
PALMER

"Believable characters that tug at heartstrings
and God's power to change hearts and
lives is beautifully depicted."
—*Romantic Times BOOKreviews* on
"Christmas in My Heart"

"Catherine Palmer…understands hurts as well as joys,
and portrays them authentically and insightfully."
—Randy Alcorn, bestselling author of *Deadline*

Praise for
JILLIAN HART

"A sweet book with lovable characters that have
problems to overcome with the help of faith and the
power of true love."
—*Romantic Times BOOKreviews* on *Homespun Bride*

"Jillian Hart conveys heart-tugging emotional struggles
and the joy of remaining open to the Lord's leading."
—*Romantic Times BOOKreviews* on *Sweet Blessings*

"These sweet and gentle romances offer the same rich
detail and charming characters readers have come to love
in her other works."
—*The Romance Reader's Connection* on
Heaven Knows and Jillian's other works

CATHERINE PALMER

JILLIAN HART

A Merry Little Christmas

Steeple
Hill®

Published by Steeple Hill Books™

STEEPLE HILL BOOKS

Steeple
Hill®

ISBN-13: 978-0-373-78632-9
ISBN-10:   0-373-78632-8

A MERRY LITTLE CHRISTMAS

Copyright © 2006 by Harlequin Books S.A.

The publisher acknowledges the copyright holders of the
individual works as follows:

UNTO US A CHILD...
Copyright © 2006 by Catherine Palmer

CHRISTMAS, DON'T BE LATE
Copyright © 2006 by Jill Strickler

CONTENTS

UNTO US A CHILD…

Catherine Palmer

* * *

For the Huber family, a living testimony of
obedience to Christ's command to love
"the least of these"…and most especially for
Tobias Huber. May God bless you all.

For unto us a child is born, unto us a son is given: and the government shall be upon his shoulder: and his name shall be called Wonderful, Counsellor, the Mighty God, the everlasting Father, the Prince of Peace.

—*Isaiah 9:6*

I was a stranger, and you invited me into your home…I assure you, when you did it to one of the least of these my brothers and sisters, you were doing it to me!

—*Matthew 25:35, 40*

Chapter One

Springfield, Missouri

The gentleman stepped into Dr. Lara Crane's office, folded his hands politely and made an announcement. "I have had a smashing time."

Lara's heart stumbled as she rose from her chair to greet the African student. "Tell me what happened, Peter."

"The situation began when I drove my car around the corner of the university library. At the moment of turning, I observed another automobile. Both were traveling very slowly, because the law allows driving at only ten miles per hour on the campus. Just then, I noticed that the other automobile was in the same lane as mine. This was when I heard the unpleasant sound of the two cars bumping together. The police arrived quickly and then an ambulance, and everyone is well."

"I'm so glad you weren't hurt, Peter."

His mouth broadened into a wide smile that brightened the glow of his smooth chocolate skin. "God is good. The bonnet of my car was pushed in, but yet, it drives quite well."

Letting out the breath she had been holding, Lara assumed a stern expression—one she was forced to wear far too often as director of the International Student Program at Reynolds University. "Peter, it's only November, and this is your third accident since you came to Missouri. The government is likely to take away your driver's license. You may even face deportation back to Kenya."

"This is why I have come to see you, Dr. Crane. You will assist me."

"I can't help you drive, Peter. You're going to have to remember to stay in the right lane." She held up her hand to illustrate. During her two-year stint with a hunger relief agency in Africa, Lara had learned to communicate with a mixture of hand signals and language. Even talking to competent English speakers like Peter Muraya, she continued the practice.

"I realize that in Kenya, people drive on the left side of the road," she told him. "But here in Missouri, you must stay on the right."

"Yes, even when turning a corner."

"*Especially* when turning a corner." She shook her head. "Did the police write you a ticket?"

"Not at all. The other car was not harmed in the collision. The driver was a very kind man, and he said he would not pursue me."

"You hit someone head-on, but the other car wasn't damaged? How can that be?"

"It was a strong car. This was the type of automobile named for that kind of bird which can fly without any sign of movement in the wings." Peter gestured animatedly, attempting to outline the shape of the mystery vehicle as well as demonstrating the flight of the unnamed bird. "The wings cannot be seen. It is a small bird that prefers to eat only nectar—"

"A hummingbird." A young man with a mop of dark brown hair breezed through the open door of Lara's small office and dropped his textbooks on her desk. "He hit a Hummer."

Lara's mouth dropped open. "Peter, you ran into a...one of those big..." Now she was gesturing again.

"A Hummer," the younger man explained. "That's what he hit. I'm not surprised there was no damage. Those things are built like tanks."

Lara shifted her attention away from the Kenyan student. "And you are...?"

"Daniel Maddox." Instead of offering his hand, he held out a yellow flyer he had pulled off a campus bulletin board. "Sorry to cut in on your conversation, Dr. Crane, but I'm on my way to class. Hey, do you still need help? This notice says you're looking for places to put international students. I've got an extra house."

Wearing a faded sweatshirt, baggy jeans and a sweat-stained ball cap, Daniel Maddox didn't look as if he could afford even one house, let alone have an extra to share. But with ten years' experience at the university, Lara had learned to be wary of appearances. A man might claim to be the son of an African prince yet be unable to pay his tuition. A girl might appear to have stepped out of an Asian slum, then turn around and buy herself a sports car. A student could enter the university with nothing more than a GED and earn a degree with honors in three years. Another student could arrive with top scores and bomb out in one semester.

"An extra house," Lara said, stepping around her desk. "You want to explain that?"

"It's a guest cottage out back by the pool," Daniel said. "Two bedrooms, kitchen, bathroom—the whole nine yards. Our house isn't far from campus. I walk to class every day. I bet my dad would agree to it. Probably wouldn't even charge much."

The young man's bright blue eyes were glowing as Lara stood and held out her hand. "I don't think we've met. I'm Dr. Lara Crane. This is Peter Muraya."

"Hey, Pete." Daniel tipped his cap at the Kenyan and gave both of them a firm handshake. "I'm a freshman at Reynolds, Dr. Crane. I'm carrying a lot of hours, and I don't have time for much on-campus stuff, so that's how come you haven't seen me."

"Your last name is Maddox. There's an architectural firm in town—"

"That's my dad. Jeremiah Maddox, but he's cooler than people say. I know what you're thinking. There was that whole deal about him putting up those condos. He's been attacked for not caring about historical preservation because he tore down that old building. But that's not it. His critics don't understand how things work in cities like Springfield."

"I see." Lara vaguely recalled a series of newspaper

articles portraying the Maddox firm in a negative light, but she didn't remember the details.

"Daniel, you are correct," Peter Muraya spoke up. "A city's infrastructure is complicated. Some old buildings may be preserved for their historical value, yet one must be willing to make way for the new."

The younger man grinned. "Yeah. Like if the building is falling down and the foundation is cracked, sometimes you have to come up with another solution."

"I believe your father is a good man," Peter said. "Please tell him that I will be happy to live in your cottage near the swimming pool."

"Now just a minute," Lara cut in. "Daniel, you need to talk to your father and see what he thinks about renting the guesthouse. I do have several students still looking for housing, and if the lease is acceptable, I'd be happy to take a look at the place."

"Awesome." A grin spread across Daniel's face. "Hey, you don't suppose you could get us a girl student, do you? Like from Norway or Sweden? Or how about France?"

Lara couldn't hold back her smile. "Doubtful. Most of the international student body at Reynolds comes to us from Africa and Asia. We have a few South Americans and Europeans, but not many."

"Okay, that was just a thought." Daniel's cheeks were suddenly flushed. He picked up his books and began backing out of the office.

"I am from Kenya," Peter Muraya said. "Would I be acceptable to you for residing at the cottage?"

"Yeah, I guess. I mean…sure."

Lara followed Daniel to the door. "I appreciate your

interest in helping out. If you want to meet our students, why don't you drop by the I-House sometime? We have activities going on nearly every evening, and we're always looking for tutors and language facilitators. Our two freshmen from Argentina—Alejandra and Maria Elena—were asking me about that last night."

Daniel's face lit in a smile. "I might do that. All right, see ya."

Before Lara could say her own goodbye, Daniel Maddox had set off down the hall and disappeared around a corner. She wondered if he would be back. Turning to Peter Muraya, Lara said, "Now about this smash…"

Jeremiah peered over the toes of his socks at the football game on the TV across the room. Stretched out in his favorite leather chair, feet propped on an ottoman, he relished his one stress-free evening of the week. With a laptop open on the table by his right arm, he could keep an eye on incoming e-mails and jot an occasional note to himself. A mug of hot chocolate at his left hand and a bowl of popcorn balanced on his stomach rounded out the perfect picture of relaxation.

"Hey, Dad." Jeremiah's son Daniel entered his peripheral vision. "Can me and Benjamin talk to you for a sec?"

"Benjamin and I," Jeremiah corrected absently. "Did you see that hit? The guy's gonna be asking for the license plate number of the truck that ran over him."

"It's about the guest cottage." Daniel plopped down on the ottoman, blocking half the television screen from view. "Me and…Ben and I were thinking we could rent it to an international student. They need houses, and I met this guy Peter who'd had a fender bender with a Hummer, you know? And he seemed like a good guy. So what do you think?"

"Yeah." Benjamin dropped onto the other half of the ottoman as a commercial interrupted the ball game. "You know how Dan started working as a leader with our youth group at church? Because he's in college and all that?"

"Yes, I know," Jeremiah said. He was proud of his older son's initiative in helping out—though he suspected some of the motivation came from Daniel's girlfriend being a high school senior who still participated in youth group activities.

"So, anyway," Benjamin went on, "Dan had us do this project where we read through the four Gospels and wrote down all the commands of Jesus."

His brother nodded. "I had an idea about putting Christ's commands in writing—all together in one list— so we could look at them. And remember how He said if you have two coats, you should give one of them away?"

"Our youth minister challenged us with that," Benjamin continued. "We're supposed to try to obey a command and then report on what we did. It's an assignment. So when Dan saw the flyer about needing houses for international students, he talked to the guy in charge—"

"It's a lady," Daniel clarified.

"Because when you think about it, we have two houses. The guest cottage is just sitting there empty. So, can we do it?"

Jeremiah tugged his attention from the wedge of television screen still in view and focused on his sons. At seventeen and nineteen, Benjamin and Daniel rarely demanded much of his time these days. A high school senior, Benjamin was Mr. Social—active in the church youth group, the art club, the student council and several other activities. Benjamin hung out with a group of teenagers who regularly filled the basement with the aroma of pizza and smelly sneakers. Daniel was a freshman physics major at Reynolds University, taking a full load of difficult courses, assisting the youth minister and spending what little free time he had with his girlfriend. Both boys owned cars, stayed fairly well-groomed, made decent grades and kept their father in a state of only mild agitation. It could be worse.

"Did you say someone ran into a Hummer?" Jeremiah asked.

"Peter. The African guy." Daniel frowned. "Dad, would you just listen to us? It's about the guest cottage. Why don't we rent it out?"

"We don't need the money," Jeremiah said. The string of commercials had ended, and the game was starting up again. "Renting is a major headache. If people don't own a place, they won't take care of it. You should see some of the buildings in this city. Nightmares."

"It's not for the money," Benjamin said. "It's like, 'I was a stranger, and you took me in.' Doing what Jesus commanded, Dad."

"I do what Jesus said," Jeremiah told his sons. "I've given ten percent of my income to the church ever since I started the firm. That's a significant amount of money. It goes to maintaining the church buildings, paying the staff, supporting missionaries and a dozen other good works. I'm sure strangers are taken care of in many different ways. You guys are a part of what I do, and you always have been, so you're covered."

"What do you mean *covered?*" Benjamin asked.

"I mean you're off the hook. I'm handling everything. When you get full-time jobs, you can choose how you want to manage your financial obligations. As a Christian, I believe I'm supposed to tithe, so I do. And that's all you need to know."

"But, Dad, we're talking about the guest cottage," Daniel said. "Hey, Ben—grab the remote."

His brother snatched the television control and flicked off the TV, while Daniel snapped the laptop shut.

"Wait a minute now!" Jeremiah sat up, spilling popcorn all over the chair. "Give me that thing. This is my one night to relax, guys! Now look at this mess."

"Just pay attention for a minute, Dad." Daniel dropped a yellow leaflet into Jeremiah's lap. "The university needs housing for international students. We have an extra house. We should let them use it."

Benjamin tapped the flyer. "The Bible says if you've been given a lot, then a lot will be required of you."

"And I just told you that I'm handing over ten percent of every dollar I make." Jeremiah picked up fistfuls of popcorn and began tossing them back into the bowl.

"Yeah, and you just budget it each month and write out a check."

"Daniel, you're making it sound like squirrel feed. It's sizable. Both of you do a lot for the church, too. You go on mission trips, you help out with youth group projects, all that. Now I want to watch the football game. Benjamin, give me the remote."

"First agree to rent the cottage." Benjamin held up the remote and dangled it like a carrot in front of a horse, just out of reach. "Do unto others. Go the extra mile. You know the verses just as well as we do, Dad. C'mon, say yes."

"Is this about girls?" Jeremiah demanded. "Because the basement is your designated space, and I'm not hosting pool parties for some—"

"A lot of the international students are your age, Dad. They're mostly from Africa and Asia." Daniel took the remote from his brother and gave it back to their father. "We just thought it would be a way to do something good. If you have extra, you're supposed to share it…. Oh, never mind. Come on, Ben. He doesn't get it."

"Whoa, now." Resisting the urge to turn on the television, Jeremiah set the popcorn bowl on the side table and studied his sons. Almost mirror images of himself, they stared back—blue eyes, dark hair, a take-no-prisoners outlook on life. They wanted something from him, and Jeremiah wasn't about to ignore them now, not after all they had been through together.

When the boys were seven and nine, their mother had vanished the week before Christmas, leaving him to pick up the pieces and try to rebuild a family. After moving to Oregon to start over with another man, Jeremiah's former wife sent her sons birthday and Christmas cards, called now and then, even mailed money when she could. But she never saw her children again. After all this time, it was still inconceivable to

Jeremiah that the woman he had loved and married could abandon her own offspring. That he had failed totally as a husband. That his wife's rejection of their family was so complete.

Years of struggle had left their mark, but Jeremiah was determined not to become bitter. He focused on his sons and his career—and he would dare anyone to question his success in both arenas. If he left a legacy at all, it wouldn't be the award-winning buildings that dotted the metropolitan centers of nearly every major city in the Midwest. It wouldn't be an architectural firm ranked among the most profitable and successful in the region. It certainly wouldn't be the sprawling stone house with its swimming pool, guest cottage and four-car garage he had designed, built and lived in for the past eight years. It would be these boys. These two fine young men in whom Jeremiah had invested his time, his money, and—most of all—his love.

Jeremiah looked at them now, their earnest expressions, their pent-up frustration. Letting out a long breath, he leaned back in his chair. "If it means that much to you, fine. Go talk to the person in charge of the program, this—" he glanced down at the flyer "—this Dr. Crane. See if the university would even be interested in putting a student in our guest cottage. We'll look into it, and see if we can help out in one way or another."

"He's gonna try to weasel out," Benjamin told his brother. "That's how he talks when he's leaving loop-holes."

"Don't worry," Daniel said. He set the bowl of popcorn back in his father's lap. "We'll win this one."

As they sauntered out of the room, Jeremiah crossed his legs, turned back to the game and dipped his hand into the popcorn. His sons successfully outmaneuvered him now and then. But only when he chose to hand them the victory flag.

Jeremiah pulled his BMW into its space in the garage and let his head drop back against the headrest. A long night of work lay ahead of him, and both boys' cars were home. That meant the basement would probably be full. And loud. Teenagers would be running up and down the stairs, baking pizzas, letting friends into the house, playing music and video games at loud volume. It was a school night, but so close to the Thanksgiving break that the teachers had all but given up assigning homework.

Lifting his briefcase from the car floor, he thought of the board meeting the following morning. Ever since the firm's clash with historic preservationists a couple of years back, everyone was spooked. Nowadays, when an old building was scheduled for demolition, the board went through the paperwork with a fine-tooth comb.

In this project, Jeremiah was working with a developer to convert a defunct shoe factory in downtown St. Louis into loft apartments. A high-class project with excellent funding, it promised to enhance the city's riverfront. The firm had worked hard on the design, and Jeremiah had spearheaded the effort to keep as much of the building's original features intact as possible. But with the board arriving in the morning, he was probably going to be up most of the night preparing to defend his plan.

"Yo, Dad!" Daniel bounced a basketball around the corner of the garage. "You're here!"

That ought to be fairly obvious, Jeremiah thought as he stepped out of the garage. Didn't his older son have a late class on Tuesday afternoons?

"He's home, Ben!" Daniel called. "Over here!"

Benjamin danced into the open. "Hey, Dad. Wanna shoot some hoops with us?"

As he looked at his sons, the tension in Jeremiah's shoulders eased. Dressed in gray sweatpants and T-shirts, they were a picture of health and wholesomeness. These were two good kids. Sure, Benjamin had spent a little time in the principal's office in grade school for acting up. And Daniel had made some unwise choices, including a girlfriend a few years before. Neither boy was perfect by a long shot. But they were turning out all right. He couldn't be prouder.

"I've got a big meeting tomorrow morning," he told them. "That St. Louis shoe factory deal is on the table."

"Aw, just half an hour," Benjamin pleaded. "C'mon, Dad!"

"Yeah, Dad."

Daniel tossed the ball to his father. Jeremiah caught it with one hand and dribbled for a moment before rifling it back to his son. Dropping his briefcase on the driveway, he shrugged out of his suit coat, rolled up the sleeves of his starched white shirt, loosened his tie and headed for the basketball hoop. Still wearing his tasseled loafers, he would probably fall and crack his tailbone, but so what?

"This way, Daniel," he called.

The older boy threw him the ball, and the three of
them went at it, just as they always had. Father and
sons, orange hoop on the side of the garage, air echoing
with the sound of the ball hitting the pavement and the
players grunting. Despite the November chill, they were
sweating in no time flat. Daniel spotted an opening and
put up a shot.

"Nothin' but net!" he crowed, pumping a fist.

"Look out, Dad." Benjamin scooped up the loose
ball and dribbled away from the hoop.

Jeremiah went for a steal. With a quick move, he
swatted Benjamin's dribble and turned it into his own.
Then, in two long strides, Jeremiah slam-dunked the
ball through the hoop just as a blue compact turned into
the driveway.

Lara stared in amazement as the man in business
clothes went airborne, stuffed a basketball into the net
and landed hard on the pavement. Ballpoint pens flew
from his shirt pocket. A cell phone leaped out of its
holster on his belt and skidded across the court. His
leather-soled shoes came down with a crack, and he
nearly lost his footing. But he stayed upright, high-
fiving one teenager and swatting another on the back.

This boyish, handsome man could *not* be Jeremiah
Maddox. After his son had left her office, Lara ran an
Internet search on the architect. Divorced, wealthy, a
talented designer, he had drawn the ire of every historical preservationist in the region by tearing down old
buildings and erecting new structures in their place. She
pictured Maddox as elderly, rigid and as sour as an old

lemon, and she had fully expected to dislike him. But this man's broad grin and playfulness—despite the ridiculous business getup—softened her heart.

Bringing her car to a stop in front of the massive stone home, Lara studied the gray facade, soaring slate roof, bank of multipaned windows and heavy oak door. With instinct born of experience, she instantly translated the cost of building such a structure into cauldrons of bubbling maize meal—enough to feed countless starving babies. Or fund vaccinations. Print AIDS education pamphlets. Build orphanages. Lara had spent only two years in the Third World, but the experience had forever changed her.

The man in the white shirt stooped to pick up his cell phone as she stepped out of her car. As she walked down the driveway toward the three ballplayers, she focused on the one face she recognized. "Daniel?"

"Hey, Dr. Crane!" Spotting her, he grinned. "This is my brother, Benjamin. And here's my dad, Jeremiah Maddox."

A little stunned at the disclosure that she had been so off the mark about him, Lara turned her attention to the father. "Mr. Maddox, pleased to meet you. I'm Lara Crane, director of the International Student program at Reynolds University." She held out her hand.

Dark brown hair scattered like blown hay across his forehead, sweat dripping from his chin, breath coming in heavy puffs, Jeremiah Maddox stared at their visitor. Blue eyes glittered like ice as he looked her quickly up and down, zeroed in on her lips for a moment, and then jerked his focus back to her eyes. He glanced over his shoulder at his son, and the skin between his brows furrowed.

"Daniel didn't tell me we were having company," he said. He gave Lara's hand a perfunctory shake, squeezing a little too hard, she thought.

"You told me to talk to Dr. Crane," the younger man said. "So I did. She's here to look at the guest cottage."

"Yeah, Dad." Benjamin gave the basketball in his hands a bounce. "We asked you the other day, remember? You said it would be okay."

"I said I would consider it."

A muscle flickered in Jeremiah's jaw, and Lara realized this whole event had caught him by surprise. Clearly his sons wanted a student to move into the extra house on the property. But why? And how could she make sure the experience was successful for all concerned? Not every American family blended well with an international student. Lara had run into explosive situations, and she didn't want to risk a mistake.

Jeremiah Maddox, with his starched shirt and cell phone holster, gave the impression of someone caught up in the pursuit of money and success. Someone who might not adapt well to a challenging living situation. He was a controller. She saw that right off the bat. And being caught off guard by his sons was not making him happy.

Tempted to head straight back to her car, she studied Daniel and Benjamin Maddox. Though they shared their father's square jaw, dark good looks and piercing blue eyes, both boys were softer somehow. Needy? Vulnerable? Something inside Lara wanted to reach out to them.

"Perhaps I should explain the situation," she told their father. "Reynolds University lacks enough housing to meet the demand. Even this late in the semester, some of our international students are living in motels or in seriously inadequate apartments."

"Why aren't they in dorms?" Jeremiah asked.

"Most are older than the traditional dormitory resident. Also, our international scholars tend to be extremely focused on their studies. They hold down part-time employment, and they need their sleep…more sleep than dorm life generally offers. I'm sure you know teenagers tend to keep late hours." She gave Jeremiah a smile, but he didn't return it.

Continuing the spiel she usually gave to prospective hosts, Lara realized that what little goodwill she had felt toward this basketball-playing father was quickly vanishing. "The university provides the International House for socialization experiences," she told him. "Most of the students in our program live in off-campus housing."

"I went by the I-House, Dad," Daniel spoke up. "It's great. They've got art on the walls from all over the world. They have a tutoring program to help the international students with their classes, because English is a barrier for a lot of them. Some of the I-students will teach classes in their language. Did you know that in Congo the people speak French?"

"That's great, Daniel, but listen, I have an important meeting tomorrow." Jeremiah's expression went from warm to positively chilly as he turned from his son to Lara. "Maybe you could call me sometime next week to discuss this matter, Dr. Crane. I have a lot of work I need to do tonight, and I'm pretty much tied up the rest of the week."

"We'll show her the guest cottage," Benjamin volunteered. "It's got a lot of room."

"More than you'd think from the front," Daniel added. "Dad designed it that way."

"Sounds wonderful. I'd love to see it." Lara focused on the two young men. "This won't take but a few minutes, Mr. Maddox. I need to know what you'd like to charge for rent. We have a standard agreement form."

"Now just a minute—"

"Come on, Dad." Daniel's brow furrowed exactly the way his father's had. "We have an extra house, and it's empty."

"We can't say no," Benjamin chimed in.

"You're a couple of con artists," Jeremiah muttered. "All right. I've got the keys. Follow me, Dr. Crane."

"One second." Lara gestured toward her car. "I'd appreciate it if Peter Muraya could see the place, too. Peter and his family."

"His what?"

The slender Kenyan stepped out of the car and beamed at Jeremiah Maddox. "Good evening, sir," he said as he helped a lovely young woman from the backseat. "May I present to you my wife, Tabitha Muraya?"

"Good evening, sir." Tabitha gave a shy smile as she leaned into the car and helped a skinny little boy clamber out. In a moment, Peter took the shoulders of the boy and planted him in front of Jeremiah.

"This is my son Wisdom who has seven years of age," he said proudly. Then he placed a second child beside the first. "My son Justice is five years old."

Tabitha Muraya emerged one last time with a

blanket-wrapped bundle in her arms. She drew aside the corner of the knitted blue cover to expose a round face with cheeks like warm chocolate muffins, a pair of bright brown eyes, and a wide toothless grin.

"And this," Peter Muraya said, "is Tobias."

Chapter Two

Five. Jeremiah counted them. One, two, three, four, five. Five people on his driveway looking at him with expectant faces, shining eyes, eager smiles—as though he were Santa Claus.

"Oh, and they do have a dog," Lara Crane said. "Wisdom and Justice found it in a garbage bin and brought it home. It's just a puppy."

A *dog*. Jeremiah rubbed his temples. Suddenly he felt like a two-ton weight had dropped on his shoulders. He glanced out of the corner of his eye at his sons. They wore the exact same expression as the Muraya family.

Please, Dad, please. He could almost hear them pleading. It was like the time they just *had* to have a toy Millennium Falcon from the *Star Wars* collection. Or a trip to Six Flags amusement park. Or a basketball goal mounted on the side of the garage. The desire for any number of things had made his sons act as if their lives depended on getting whatever it was.

But this was no toy or vacation trip. These were human beings. Five of them. And a dog.

He looked at Lara Crane. This was her fault. She had somehow coerced Daniel. Jeremiah's son—always a sucker for an appeal from a pretty woman—would give away his last dollar if he thought it might help a lady in need. Tall, attractive, with a mop of shoulder-length strawberry blonde curls, the program director looked too young to have an advanced degree. Probably only in her midthirties, the woman would have no realistic idea what she was asking of him. No doubt she had come into her position all starry-eyed and full of goodwill. She probably expected people to fall all over themselves with joy over the privilege of housing her international students.

"I can't have a dog on the property," Jeremiah told her. "My landscaping was just redone this summer—"

"With a new fence around the pool and another one around the backyard," Benjamin spoke up. "It would be cool to have a dog."

"We've always wanted a dog," Daniel said. The light of pleading in his blue eyes was growing stronger by the minute. "Dad, I didn't realize there was a whole family when I brought it up to Dr. Crane. But why not?"

"The cottage only has two bedrooms, for one thing."

"The Murayas have been living in a single motel room for three months." Lara Crane was insidiously leading Jeremiah's sons toward the family. "Two bedrooms, a kitchen and a bathroom will feel like a mansion. I'm sure they'll take good care of your property, Mr. Maddox."

Jeremiah couldn't help but follow the group, tagging

along behind, hoping he could somehow put a stop to the inevitable meeting. And then it was too late. Benjamin knelt and shook hands with the two little boys. Daniel lifted the baby out of his mother's arms. Peter Muraya laughed with delight as his sons began to cavort happily around the group. Tabitha covered her mouth with her hand and giggled.

"Dad, look at this baby!" Daniel said, swinging toward his lagging father. "He's a chunk."

"Here, give me the cottage keys!" Benjamin swiped the ring from Jeremiah's hand and beckoned. "Come on, everyone. It's right back here. You'll love it. There's room for everyone, and more!"

"Yeah," Daniel said. "Here, Dad. Take this little guy."

Before Jeremiah could protest, Daniel lifted Tobias Muraya into his arms. The warm, slightly damp and unexpectedly heavy bundle emitted the fragrance of talcum powder and baby oil. With Jeremiah's sons holding the hands of Wisdom and Justice, the young African couple hurried off down the driveway and around the garage.

"The Murayas are from Kenya," Lara Crane said, pausing long enough for the others to go on ahead.

Jeremiah tried to think where Kenya was situated on the continent of Africa. Then he realized he didn't care. "I appreciate your work," he told the woman, "but I really can't have a whole family living in the guest cottage."

"Peter Muraya is pursuing his doctorate in civil engineering. He hopes to return to Kenya and help rebuild its sagging infrastructure."

"That's great, but five people..." Jeremiah looked

down at the blue bundle in his arms. Solemn brown eyes in a small round face stared up at him. Eyes like chocolate bonbons shone, encircled by long, curling black lashes.

I'm holding a baby, Jeremiah thought. I haven't done this for eighteen years. I don't hold babies. I'm an architect. I design buildings.

"Tabitha is a great mother." Lara Crane's voice broke into his reverie. "She and Peter spent several years apart while he studied for his graduate degree. She practically raised Wisdom and Justice by herself. Then the family was able to be reunited, and nine months later, along came Tobias. He's been a great blessing to all the Murayas."

As if on cue, the baby's face suddenly broke into a broad grin. That was when Jeremiah saw it. A tooth. One tiny white tooth barely poked through the gum on Tobias's lower jaw. Instinctively, Jeremiah placed his index finger on the tooth…and sure enough. There it was. The baby's first tooth. Tobias let out a gurgle and clamped down.

"Ow!" Jerking away his finger, Jeremiah looked up sheepishly at Lara Crane.

"They do bite," she said.

"I'd forgotten. It's been a long time."

"Kids grow up fast. Your sons are great, by the way. I was very impressed with Daniel when he visited my office the other day. I think Wisdom and Justice will enjoy being around older boys. I'm sure it will be a positive influence—both ways."

Jeremiah regarded Lara. He now saw that she had green eyes and a sprinkling of freckles across her nose.

Evidently, she had tried to conceal the freckles with makeup. It hadn't worked. Despite his determination to resent the woman and her interference in his life, he couldn't deny the delightful effect of those freckles. Dr. Lara Crane was downright cute.

"So, how many international students live at *your* house?" he asked her.

"The university doesn't allow the students to live with anyone except their own family members. We do pair those in our program with area residents for fellowship and the benefit of cultural exchange, but we've found it doesn't work well to place students in private homes."

"This situation wouldn't be against the rules?"

"Your guest cottage is a separate dwelling." She turned her shoulder on him and started strolling after the group. "Mr. Maddox, you really won't need to have much interaction with the family if you'd prefer to keep a distance. If I were you, though, I would welcome the opportunity to introduce my sons to another culture."

"If you were me, you'd know how hard it is to raise kids without taking on a whole extra family. How many children do you have, Dr. Crane?"

"Please call me Lara. I'm single, but I spent the best two years of my life working for a hunger relief agency in Sudan. It changed my whole perspective."

"Maybe so, but you can't possibly understand my situation." Jeremiah accompanied Lara as she rounded the corner of the garage and headed down a path leading to the cottage. "I've had sole custody of my sons for the past ten years, and it hasn't been easy."

"Peter Muraya would understand that kind of challenge. The Murayas have been trying to raise their children on two different continents and with a very limited income. Peter is not from a wealthy family in Kenya. His father was able to pay school fees only for his oldest son. Peter has four younger brothers and two sisters. So he is the focus of his parents' dreams and hopes. He was able to get academic scholarships and grants to pay for his schooling, but he also holds down a job as a janitor at Reynolds. In Kenya, Tabitha crocheted bedspreads for a women's cooperative. She was able to be home with her children and work at the same time. But here, her visa won't allow her to have a job."

"Wait a minute. You're telling me that a Ph.D. candidate in civil engineering is working as a janitor?" Jeremiah found it hard to imagine. "And supporting a family of five?"

"The Murayas will do whatever it takes to succeed," she said. "It would be helpful, Mr. Maddox, if you could keep the rent low."

"But I haven't agreed to this. I need to think it over." The baby in his arms began to wriggle. He looked down in time to see the bright brown eyes fill with tears as the little mouth scrunched into an unhappy frown. Jeremiah knew from experience that an ear-piercing scream was about to be loosed. He held Tobias toward Lara.

"Here, you take him. He's not happy."

"Jiggle him," she shot back. "I need to make sure the cottage is suitable."

She stepped through the guesthouse door just as Tobias Muraya began to howl. *Great,* Jeremiah thought.

A board meeting. Two teenagers. A wet, crying baby. An unexpected family. And a puppy.

This was *not* going to happen.

While checking the miniblinds for safety features, Lara peeked through the window at Jeremiah Maddox. He was holding Tobias at an awkward angle while the baby waved his tiny arms and bawled, volume increasing by the second.

She watched with amusement. Such a smart, sophisticated, handsome man. And so superior in his views. *I can't have a dog on the property. My landscaping was just redone this summer.* Well, la-di-dah. Welcome to the real world, Mr. Jeremiah Maddox.

Tabitha Muraya had scampered out the front door the moment she heard her baby's cries. Now she was lifting Tobias into her arms, balancing him over her shoulder, patting his back, rearranging the blue blanket. She spoke briefly to Jeremiah before hurrying back into the cottage. He stood in silence, then hung his head and rubbed the back of his neck.

Lara had to give the man credit for raising two fine young men. Daniel and Benjamin clearly had a heart for helping others, and they were getting a huge kick out of playing tag with Wisdom and Justice. This cottage would be perfect for the Murayas. It was clean, dry and roomy enough for the family to manage beautifully. Peter could continue his studies in a much better atmosphere, and his older sons wouldn't even have to change schools.

Outside, Jeremiah let out a deep breath and looked up into the sky. She wondered if he was praying and hoped so. It would be a shame if a man who had so much going for him kept it all to himself. Lara had learned the hard way that following Christ meant taking on a servant attitude, and she wondered why that was so hard for some people to understand.

God had given Jeremiah a great opportunity to help the Muraya family, she thought as she watched him start toward the cottage. As he stepped through the door, she let the blind fall back into place and gave the couch a pat. Solid. Top-quality furniture, a fully equipped kitchen, two large bedrooms and a bath with a jetted tub. This was considerably better than her own cramped little bungalow.

Jeremiah crossed the room, took Lara's arm and began to lead her away from the hubbub of the running kids and the fussy baby. As he moved, he lowered his head so it was near her ear and spoke in a muted voice. "Listen, I can't do this. It's a worthy cause, and I'll contribute financially to your program. But I just can't have a family of five living in my backyard."

Lara halted and looked into his face. Seeking privacy, Jeremiah had propelled her into an alcove with a bay window that faced the yard and the pool. He stood less than a foot away from her, his presence dominating the small space. It was appropriate and quiet for them to speak there, and yet for some reason, Lara felt totally thrown off balance. Suddenly she couldn't remember the last time she'd been so close to a man. For what felt like ten years, it was all she could think about. This man in his starched white shirt. His dark hair and blue eyes. A trace of cologne mixed with perspiration from playing basketball with his boys. His warm hand on her arm, cupping her elbow, fingers pressing against her skin.

She tried to breathe and couldn't get the air to go down. Biting her lower lip, she fought for control. Okay, this was ridiculous. She had just broken off a short-term relationship with a man she'd met at church, and they had certainly been this near each other. She regularly shook hands with her foreign students and sometimes met with them alone in her office. It wasn't as though she had isolated herself from the male gender.

"Did you hear what I said?" Jeremiah asked. His voice rumbled from somewhere down in his chest. "I don't believe I can do the family justice."

"Justice," she managed, "is five years old. He needs a home. You have an extra house."

"And I have two kids of my own to look after. Listen, Dr. Crane…Lara…teenagers run around here all the time. They're in and out of the driveway, the house, the backyard, the pool. I can't be responsible for protecting these folks. The legal ramifications are immense. It's just not wise."

"Wisdom is seven." She was breathing again, her blood pumping and fire flowing back into her chest. "Tobias is five months old. You have room for them. You cannot say no."

"Yes, I can. This is my guest cottage. It's reserved for my visitors. People stay here sometimes."

"So put your visitors up in your house. I doubt you and your two sons take up every square inch of that monster across the yard."

"Monster?" He leaned closer, his face coming within

an inch of hers. "I designed that house. I built that house. That is *my* house."

"*My* house, *my* visitors, *my* backyard, *my* landscaping, *my* guest cottage. Are those things really important to you, Mr. Maddox?" She set her hands on her hips. "Can you just tell me what matters most in your life?"

"That should be obvious. My sons are more important to me than anything else. I've spent my adult life taking care of them and raising them to be decent, productive young men."

"And you've succeeded so well that they want to reach out and help others. It wouldn't matter to Daniel and Benjamin if you stashed the odd guest or two in your house so the Murayas could live here."

"I don't have *odd* guests. I have *normal* guests and *normal* kids. And I don't intend to raise my sons in any kind of unpredictable, potentially troublesome atmosphere. With a situation like this, who knows what could happen?" He glanced out of the alcove as Wisdom went tearing by, Daniel in hot pursuit. "These people are from another country, another culture. I don't know how to handle them. I don't have time to deal with problems that might crop up."

"*These* people are a wonderful family who have been coping with very difficult circumstances. People are people, Mr. Maddox, no matter where they come from. Some are kindhearted, warm, generous and godly. Others are cold, selfish and mean-spirited. The Murayas would fall into the first category."

"And I suppose you think I rank with the cruel despots of the world?"

"You're not showing much heart."

"I don't have much heart, okay?" He turned away, staring out the window. When he spoke again, his voice was stilted. "I love my sons. Ten years ago almost to the day, their mother walked out on us. I won't do anything—" he turned to her "—*anything* that might hurt them. I have built a family. A home. A world that is safe and right for those boys. Things are as whole as they can be for two kids without a mother. You have to understand. I won't take risks with that. It's too precious to me."

Lara could hear the pain in his words. She reached out and laid her hand on his arm. "Jeremiah, your sons are almost grown, and you've done well. But Daniel and Benjamin are getting ready to step out into a world beyond the one you've created for them. It's a place you can't control. It's huge and needy and filled with risk. They want to see that world, and the Murayas are part of it. Give this experience to your boys. Give a home to this family. It will be all right. I promise."

When he looked back at her, Lara could see that her arguments had prevailed. But something in his eyes kept her from feeling victorious.

"I have an important meeting tomorrow morning," he said. "My firm is designing the renovation of a factory in St. Louis. I'll be out of town off and on until next summer, and I can't keep tabs on all this. So, you will. You'll come here twice a week to check on the Murayas. You'll make sure they're doing well. And you'll see that my property is cared for, and my sons are having a good experience. Otherwise, the family is gone."

Lara's mouth dropped open. "Twice a week? I can't do

that! Do you realize how many students I supervise? I have an entire program to manage, and I can't possibly—"

"You promised. You said it would be all right, and I'm holding you to that. Twice a week. Send me an e-mail update each time you check on the family. Agree to these conditions, and the rent is free. Peter can pay the utilities." He started to step out of the alcove.

She caught his arm. "You are the most controlling, self-absorbed—"

"Trying to weasel out of your promise, Lara?" He swung around, blue eyes blazing. "Because I don't deal well with people who break their vows."

"I'm not your wife. Get over it."

"Do we have a deal or not?"

She pursed her lips, biting back the words on the tip of her tongue. "Fine. Twice a week. And you need to ask the Murayas for a damage deposit and make them pay a nominal rent. People do best when they earn their way. I can think of only one freebie that was ever worth having."

"What's that?"

"Read your Bible," she muttered, shouldering past him out of the alcove. "Peter, Tabitha? Mr. Maddox and I have reached an agreement. You can move in this weekend."

If Lara Crane was a Christian, she was the prickliest one Jeremiah had ever met. Also, definitely the cutest. He wished he could stop thinking about the way her green eyes had sparked when she told him to *get over it.* As he drove home from his office in downtown Springfield that Friday evening, he pondered her words once again.

He had thought he *was* over it.

In the ten years since his wife left, Jeremiah had re-focused his life. He had analyzed where he went wrong, and he had made every effort to correct his obvious failings. During his marriage, he had been extremely self-centered—choosing golf, his work, his old college buddies, over spending time with his family. He hadn't helped his wife much with the boys. He had argued against her desire to start a home-based business selling toys online. He had resented the hours she spent on the computer, but he preferred watching television to talking with her. Certainly he hadn't been interested in listening to every detail of her life at the end of a long day. She bored him, and he made little effort to conceal it.

Now he was a different man, Jeremiah told himself. Everything he did was for his sons. He listened to their ideas. Answered their questions. Went to their sporting events and school programs. Made dinner for them almost every night. He had stopped playing golf except on business trips, and he went on as few of those as possible. He made an all-out effort to take part in things that mattered to Daniel and Benjamin.

As he pulled into the garage, Jeremiah noted that once again both boys' cars were in place. Odd for a Friday night, but he welcomed the thought of a house full of kids. He would be gone most of the following day. Electing to avoid the arrival of his new tenants, Jeremiah had scheduled an outing to an antiques mall and teahouse with a woman he had been dating for a few months. Melissa was a lovely lady, an interior designer. Like him, she was divorced with nearly grown kids.

They had met on a job and found they enjoyed each other's company. Though he hadn't seen her so regularly that she would believe his intentions were serious, he looked forward to their time together. He had promised himself he would not remarry, at least until the boys were grown, and his relationships reflected that.

At the same time, Jeremiah thought he was pretty good with women. He knew how to be kind and generous and even romantic. He rarely dwelled on his ex-wife in conversation, and he considered himself a truly reformed man. A gentleman, if that wasn't overstating it. After all, he was going to look at antiques and drink tea the next day—and if that didn't say something about how he had changed, he wasn't sure what would.

Climbing out of his car, Jeremiah heard the shout of a child as the garage door came down. The Muraya family wasn't supposed to move in until the following morning, and his plan to spend the day with Melissa would conveniently remove him from that whole event. The cry outside hadn't sounded like a teenager, though, and Jeremiah crossed to the back door. As he pulled back a curtain that covered the window, he spotted them.

Two small children raced around in circles in the yard. One of the ugliest mutts Jeremiah had ever seen ran after them, barking its fool head off. And two teenage boys tossed a football back and forth over the kids' heads as they all trampled the recently seeded lawn.

A pang of trepidation shooting through his chest, Jeremiah glanced at the guest cottage. Through the front doorway stepped a woman with a shock of strawberry blonde curls. She spotted the kids and broke into a big grin.

"No," he said out loud. "No, no, no. Not this. Not her."

Even though he had ordered Lara Crane to visit the Murayas twice a week, Jeremiah had planned to be far from home when she showed up. He didn't want to see those snapping green eyes. He didn't want to hear her challenges and accusations. What he wanted was to stop thinking about her. But here she was again. Walking right toward him in a pair of jeans, a Reynolds University sweatshirt and a baseball cap—and looking positively fetching.

"Run, Wisdom!" she sang out. "You can catch the ball! Get in front of him!"

How could a grown woman—one whom he knew to be as prickly and stiff as a cactus—look so soft and sweet all of a sudden? As she clapped her hands together and jumped up and down on her tiptoes, Jeremiah realized she was downright striking. Her golden-red hair bounced around her shoulders. Her laugh echoed through oak trees still shedding the last of their leaves in the yard. Smaller than he remembered, today she looked like a college girl, and Jeremiah wondered if he had misjudged her age. On the other hand, she was *Dr. Lara Crane,* director of a university program. She couldn't be that much younger than he.

Reaching for the doorknob, Jeremiah caught himself. He couldn't go out there. He didn't want to see her. Didn't want any part of this whole tenant-landlord thing. This was for his sons, and he planned to stay as detached as he could.

Lara cheered and applauded wildly as Justice caught a ball that Daniel had purposely thrown short. Then

Peter and Tabitha walked out of the guest cottage and studied their sons for a moment. The three adults headed toward a rusty station wagon with two mattresses protruding from the back end. Grabbing one of them, they began to wrestle the lumpy thing out onto the driveway.

"Whoa! Hold on, there!" Jeremiah called, pushing through the garage's back door and out into the yard. "There are good mattresses inside. The guest cottage already has enough beds for everyone."

The three beside the old car paused and turned to stare. As Peter recognized Jeremiah, his smile widened. "Mr. Maddox, you have come home at last! Good evening, sir."

"Good evening, sir," Tabitha echoed.

Jeremiah noted a solid round bundle tied onto the petite woman's back. Her burden rested inside a large cloth with a traditional African design, knotted over one shoulder. Wondering if this were some treasured family possession, he leaned closer. Two bright brown eyes peered at him over the edge of the fabric. Definitely a treasured possession. It was Tobias.

"Good evening, Mr. and Mrs. Muraya," Jeremiah said. He pushed his hands into his pockets to keep from touching the baby's small head with its soft curls. "Dr. Crane, we have plenty of beds. I ordered a crib for Tobias. The furniture store was supposed to deliver it and set it up two days ago."

"I noticed that. Thank you." Lara's green eyes were soft. "But Peter and Tabitha told me they would prefer to use their own things. These two mattresses are all the furniture they own, and they're concerned about keeping the house in good shape. We've moved your newer mattresses into the guest garage."

"But I'm renting the house furnished." He couldn't fathom it. Why take off good mattresses and replace them with junk? "I expect the beds and all the furniture to be used."

"These are not bad mattresses," Peter said. "And you know, we have two small boys and a baby. Not to mention the dog, which my wife insisted must stay with us."

A look of uneasiness came over Tabitha's face. She glanced away shyly. "The dog is not allowed to stand on the beds or the chairs, sir. I believe I can train him."

"But he is still a puppy, and he likes to chew things. Mr. Maddox, you have given us a good bargain on the rent for this house, and we are grateful. We believe that if we sleep on these mattresses, it will go well for us."

"No, please." Jeremiah placed a hand on the threadbare old bedding. "I'm serious now. You can put these in the garage and use the others. Please, I want you to do that. It won't matter about the dog and the children. I know how rough they can be on things."

As he spoke, the puppy—a blur of wiry brown and gray hair—bounded through the open gate, tore across a swath of damp grass and leaped up on Jeremiah. Two streaks of mud followed the furry paws down his pant legs. Before he could react, the dog had moved to greet one adult after the other with a bounce and a kiss of wet pink tongue. Peter cried out in dismay at the brown smudges on their landlord's trousers, and Tabitha gasped and clamped her hand over her mouth.

"Hey, Dad!" Daniel caught his father's attention just

in time to drill the muddy football into Jeremiah's arms. "Good catch! Oh, yeah—the Murayas needed to move in a day early. I forgot to tell you. Dr. Crane e-mailed me the other day."

Both boys came jogging over, followed closely by their smaller counterparts. Benjamin swung Justice onto his back as the puppy ran to meet them.

"This is *Mdogo*," Daniel announced, scooping the dog up in his arms. "It means *small*. Cool, huh? They haven't been here ten minutes, and I'm talking African."

"There is no language known as *African*," Peter Muraya said politely. "The national language of Kenya is Kiswahili. Sometimes we just say Swahili. Each country in Africa has a national language, and each tribe within the country has its own language. My family is of the Kikuyu tribe. So you see that Africans can have much trouble with communication."

"Yeah," Benjamin said, "but at least you get to learn different languages. Schools around here keep cutting programs like that. In Missouri, about all we can talk is American."

"Pardon me, but you speak English, not American." Peter smiled at the younger teen. "There is always much to learn, no matter where one lives."

"I can wash your suit," a low voice spoke up beside Jeremiah. "I will remove the mud from your trousers."

He looked over to find Peter's wife gazing up at him, her solemn expression mirrored in the eyes of the baby on her back. "It's not a problem," he told Tabitha. "Don't worry about it. I take my clothes to a dry cleaner. And so, uh—" he surveyed the others "—why did you change the moving date? I thought we had settled on tomorrow."

"The motel rented out their room," Lara explained. "Once the Murayas gave notice they were moving, the manager found a replacement very quickly."

"I see." Jeremiah met her green eyes and instantly regretted it. She hadn't bothered with makeup today, and her freckles were dancing wildly across her nose. Her cheeks had a bright glow, and her hair was just begging for his touch.

"Well then," he said. "I guess that's the way it is."

"Yep. Adaptability," she told him. "Life is all about being adaptable. So, you're sure about the mattresses, because I've lugged these about all I want to for one evening."

"Absolutely. We'll put them in the guest garage."

Before she could say anything else, Jeremiah set to work tugging the saggy old bedding out of the station wagon. Peter, Daniel and Benjamin joined in immediately. Before long, they had succeeded in hauling the Murayas' mattresses into the garage and returning the beds to their former place inside the cottage. As the men worked, Jeremiah stripped off his jacket and tie, and by the time the puppy had said howdy four or five more times, he was a muddy, sweating mess.

"I brought several boxes of donated food from my church pantry," Lara called out to the parade of men moving in and out of the house. She stood behind a marble-topped counter as she taught Tabitha how to use the stove and microwave. "They're in my car. If you guys could get those, we'll set up the kitchen."

Jeremiah glanced at her as he started outside again. What on earth was he doing? He had planned to build a nice blaze in the fireplace in his room, dine on leftovers from the night before and relax with a book before an early bedtime. Instead, he was dragging around bedraggled old mattresses and fending off a puppy determined to change the color of his charcoal suit to a nice shade of mud.

"Oh, by the way, Jeremiah, how was your meeting?" Lara asked when he passed her. "The one you had the other day."

He paused to think for a second. He wasn't used to anyone knowing his business. Or caring.

She clarified, "You're remodeling a shoe factory in St. Louis?"

"Yes. Fine. They approved the project." He considered following his sons back outside but paused again. "Is moving students around part of your job description?"

"About half of what I do isn't official."

"Just a freebie?" he asked.

She smiled. "The best things in life are free, or so they tell me."

"I do read the Bible, you know. I understood what you meant the other day—Christ's death on the cross, the ultimate, undeserved freebie. Is that why you do all this? Somehow trying to pay Him back?"

"That's not possible. Free is free. No repayment required."

"Then why? It's obviously more than a job."

Lara glanced at Tabitha, who was murmuring approval and awe as she inspected the contents of the kitchen cabinets. Then Lara's eyes focused on the man who stood nearby, pinning him down as she assessed him.

"You know, I've been thinking about pizza," she said. "A couple of large pepperonis. Delivered. Could you take care of that, Jeremiah?"

Chapter Three

Lara wrapped a string of melted cheese three times around her index finger and popped it into her mouth. As she drew it back out again, she caught Jeremiah Maddox watching her.

"I realize this is my third slice," she said with a trace of guilt. "I skipped lunch."

He shrugged. "Eat as much as you want."

She gave him a faint smile and glanced toward the couch, where four sets of shoulders hunched over plates of pepperoni pizza as cartoons flashed across the television screen. The boys had decided the small dining table was too crowded with adults, and the TV held more appeal than the African history lesson Peter Muraya seemed determined to share with his landlord.

Lara focused on Jeremiah again, and he was still staring. If the man wasn't calculating her pizza intake, what was he gawking at? All evening, she had noticed his eyes following her. If she was making a bed, he was putting clothing in dresser drawers…and watching her. If she was helping Tabitha put food in the refrigerator, he was setting cans in the pantry…and watching her. Did she look that bad in her jeans and ratty sweatshirt? Was it the hair or what?

"In 1963," Peter said, "Kenya finally received independence from British rule. We call this Uhuru Day. *Uhuru* means 'freedom' in Kiswahili. It is like the Fourth of July for you. A very happy time of celebration each year."

Lara nodded, trying to be polite and attentive about information she already knew. She had been in and out of Kenya several times while working for the hunger relief agency. She had also studied the country's history when she accepted the position as director of the international student program. Jeremiah downed the last of his soda and leaned back in the chair. He couldn't have been listening to much of what Peter had said. Throughout the meal he had been gnawing on pizza, answering his cell phone or scrutinizing Lara.

"Jomo Kenyatta was your first president," Jeremiah said, focusing in on Peter. "A few years ago, you changed to a multiparty system of government, I believe."

"Oh, you know about our country! Tabitha, Mr. Maddox is very knowledgeable." Peter beamed at his wife. She had put Tobias to bed a few moments before and had just rejoined them.

"This is most unusual," she said. "Few Americans understand the history of Africa."

"I minored in political science," Jeremiah told the couple. "I was interested in going to Africa at one time.

The history and geography fascinated me, but the thing that intrigued me the most was the architecture."

"Architecture?" Peter's brow furrowed deeply. "Do you speak of the Egyptian Pyramids? Or the old mosques in Mali? Africa has many things of which to boast—a long history, interesting cultures, beautiful art. But I cannot say we have much architecture that is noteworthy. Most of our early structures were built of primitive materials and have long ago vanished due to erosion, warfare or the encroachment of colonization."

Jeremiah shook his head. "No, I'm talking about round huts. Domes. You were building the most efficient structures in the world long before the modern world figured it out. A square or a rectangle isn't nearly as strong, as weather resistant or even as useful as a circle. Depending on what it's made from, a cube can easily crack, leak, burst or even collapse. The dome or cylinder shape withstands environmental pressures much longer."

"You must go to Kenya, sir," Tabitha said, her dark eyes flashing sideways at him. "The Masai tribe builds domes of sticks, mud and cow dung."

"This story will amuse you," Peter told the group. "When I was a boy, a man came to our village to assist us. He built a square tank for water containment. A cube. The sides cracked, and the rainwater ran out straight away, and we all laughed greatly at him. Next, he built a round water tank, and that catchment is still full to this very day."

"There you go," Jeremiah said.

At that pronouncement, Lara decided the landlord and his tenants were getting along fine. It was time for her to head out. She had a full Saturday planned, and she had been hoping for an early bedtime. But as she opened her mouth to bid her farewells, the cottage doorbell rang.

At the shrill sound, the puppy began to bark frantically and the baby started wailing in the bedroom. Daniel lunged for the door, nearly tripping on Benjamin, who had headed in the same direction. Justice jumped to his feet and knocked his soda onto the floor. Tabitha let out a cry of dismay and leaped toward the kitchen to grab a towel. Peter rushed to control the dog. The door blew open, and seven teenagers—all talking at once—burst into the house.

"This is it," Daniel announced proudly, "the place to be! This is Peter and Tabitha, and Wisdom and Justice."

"Hey, Mr. Maddox!" one of the girls sang out.

"It's Dr. Crane!" a boy said. "What's she doing here?"

"Let's all go over to your basement, Ben. There's not enough room here."

"Hold on. I want you to meet everyone."

"Why don't we order some more pizzas?"

"I want mushroom. No anchovies this time. I mean it."

"Cute dog! What breed is he?"

"What kind of names are Wisdom and Justice?"

Lara grabbed her purse. She was slipping into her coat when a hand clamped onto her arm. Swinging around, she saw Jeremiah Maddox—howling baby in a squirmy bundle on his shoulder—glaring at her.

"Where do you think you're going?"

"Home." She patted the baby's little round bottom. "Have fun."

"Hold on a minute. You can't abandon me here."

"You don't have to stay, either."

"Yeah, but I—" He lifted Tobias from his shoulder and pushed him at Lara. "Take this baby."

"No," she said evenly. "You picked him up. He's all yours."

"He's not mine. Nothing here is mine. I didn't ask for any of this."

"Jeremiah, we have an agreement. I will check on the Muraya family twice a week and send you a note informing you that I've been here. Otherwise, I'm out of the picture."

"But this is not okay. There's soda all over the floor. And a puppy. And—"

"And teenagers and pizza and a whole lot of fun. Enjoy!"

She waved the tips of her fingers at him and hurried toward the door. Sidestepping sprawling teenagers and somersaulting little boys, evading an anxious mother and dodging a puppy with springs in its legs, Lara made it across the room. She turned the doorknob, stepped out into the chill November air and pulled the door shut behind her.

Thank God! Looking up at the stars, she felt a ripple of blissful praise well up inside her. This was going to be great. The Lord had solved another problem. Jeremiah's boys would be wonderful for the two little Murayas, the puppy would add just enough havoc to keep things lively, Peter and Tabitha could make a happy home and Jeremiah…well, he was in for a shake-up of the tidy, comfortable world he had built for himself. Exactly what the man needed, in Lara's opinion.

She passed Peter's badly dented car and lifted up a petition that God would keep him from having any more "smashing" moments. And then she turned her prayers toward the host of other matters pressing for attention. A student from Ivory Coast had suddenly lost e-mail and phone contact with her entire extended family. Political instability in the West African nation didn't bode well. As Lara approached her car, she asked the Lord for a breakthrough in communication for the frightened young woman.

Then there was the Indian student she had spent hours with that morning. His two older brothers had breezed through Reynolds University and were working on doctorates in other states. This poor kid, on the other hand, was a lost lamb. He was failing most of his classes and in danger of losing his student visa. And then there was the young man from Brazil on a tennis scholarship who had managed to break his leg....

"Lara."

The word brought her to a halt. She knew it was Jeremiah even before she turned.

"Can I help you?" she asked.

"Yes." He stepped closer. "You can tell me why you thought it was okay to walk away the minute everything in that house started getting out of hand."

Clenched fists at his hips and the stern set of his jaw caused Lara to back into the side of her car. "I didn't walk out on you. I would never abandon anyone. I simply needed to head for home."

"You walked out of the cottage and shut the door on me."

"And I'll be back. I will check on the Murayas twice a week, as I promised."

"But you left me to take charge of that whole mess. I watched you go."

"You watched me, all right. You never stopped looking at me all night. What's your problem? Don't you trust me?"

He slid his hands into his pockets and let out a breath. "Why should I trust you, Lara? I don't trust anyone."

"Well, you should, and you can start with me. I said I would come back, and I will. I want this to be a successful placement for the Murayas. And I want you and your sons to be happy."

"You care whether we're happy?"

"Of course. I'm hoping that when the Murayas move out, you'll be willing to rent the cottage to other international students. I'm going to do everything in my power to make this work. But it's not going to be perfect, Jeremiah. They're a family with three kids and a dog. You'll have…issues."

"I don't need issues."

"It's not about what you need." She realized she was having to lift her chin to meet his eyes. "It's about the Muraya family. Life is never about *us.* It's always about *them.*"

"You don't have two sons. My life is about *us.*"

"I have forty-three students depending on me, some of them much needier and less capable than Daniel and Benjamin. Please relax. I'll come back. You can call me if you have a problem. I want this to work, and you can count on me to be here."

He gave a mirthless laugh. "Right."

"Maybe not *here.* But I'll be available. I don't live very far from you." She dug into her purse. "Take my card. It has my home address and phone number on it. Students call me all the time. Host families, too."

"Other people in town are doing this? Letting families move in with them?"

"The Murayas are your renters, that's all. But I do work to connect local families with my students in order to facilitate cultural exchange. I recruit people from churches, civic clubs, that sort of thing. I try to pair each foreign student with a family."

He was studying her card in the moonlight when the cottage door suddenly opened and kids came pouring out. In the chill night air, they raced across the drive, passing Lara and Jeremiah in their headlong dash for the back door to the main house. She noted that Wisdom and Justice had stayed with their parents.

"Yo, Dad, Dr. Crane!" Benjamin skidded to a halt in front of them. "You won't believe this. Mrs. Muraya is going to teach Dan's girlfriend and some of the others how to crochet. She makes bedspreads. Me and Dan are going to give it a try, too."

"Dan and I," Jeremiah corrected. "Did you say you're going to crochet?"

"Yeah, why not? The girls will be over here all the time!"

With a whoop, he bounded off. Lara laughed as Jeremiah shook his head. *"Girls,"* he said. "I figured there was an ulterior motive."

"See?" Lara said. "This is going to be fine, and they

don't need you around to solve everything. How much do you want to bet the Murayas have mopped up the spilled soda and put the baby back to bed? They're probably running a bath for the boys."

"Let's go check." He took her arm. "I need to give them the spare key I had made."

"Oh, but…" She suddenly found herself linked arm in arm with Jeremiah as he propelled her back down the drive toward the cottage. "But I need to get home. I have a busy day tomorrow, and there's a student from Ivory Coast who—"

"Dinner," he said. "If that baby's crying, you owe me dinner. If he's asleep, it's on me. Winner names the restaurant."

"Deal," she said.

They were still a good fifty feet from the house when Lara knew she was in trouble. Tobias was wailing like a siren. Despite the well-insulated walls and double-paned windows, the din rang clearly across the frigid air.

"You owe me, Dr. Crane," Jeremiah said. "Name your date and time."

"Thanksgiving." She turned toward him, and suddenly realized they were far too close. "We have a dinner for the international students at the I-House at noon. Everyone brings a dish from their home country. Amazing foods. Daniel and Benjamin will love it."

"Thanksgiving? We always go to my parents' house in Bolivar. It's a tradition. Turkey, dressing, football, all that."

"Bring your turkey and dressing to dinner at the I-House. Bring your parents, too. And you can teach the students how to play American football. Jeremiah, your cozy comfort zone changed the minute you agreed to rent to the Murayas. So, come see what the world has to offer."

"You're serious about this, aren't you? Are the students all you think about?"

"I think about other things. Tomorrow I'm helping rehab a house for an old woman. A couple of weeks ago, she nearly died of carbon monoxide poisoning. When social services sent people in to fix her furnace, they couldn't believe the condition of the home. So we're painting and making repairs tomorrow."

"Who's we?"

"Rehab & Renew—we call it R & R. Small joke there, because we actually work our tails off. It's a group here in Springfield. A Christian organization. It's their ministry, and I like helping out. A great change from office work. In some ways, it really is relaxing. Why don't you join us?"

He stared at her, his eyes bluer in the moonlight than she had anticipated. "What's driving you, Lara? All this helping stuff?"

"I'm a Christian."

"So am I, but I don't spend all my free time doing charity work. I take care of my family, and I write out a check for the church."

"Then you're missing the blessing."

As they reached the front door, Lara realized the cottage had gone quiet. "Wait a second," she said. "The baby's asleep. I won. You owe me dinner. Ha."

"Tomorrow," he said quickly. "Six."

"Now wait—"

"Too late, Dr. Crane. We have a date." As he was

speaking, his cell phone warbled. He reached for the holster on his belt. "Melissa?" he said into the phone, his voice softening. "Hey there. Yeah, about tomorrow…"

Unable to trust herself, Lara turned away from him and started for her car. As she slipped the key into the ignition, she shook her head in disbelief. She was *not* going on a date with Jeremiah Maddox. Who was Melissa? And why on earth did she even care?

Jeremiah drove down a street lined with dilapidated houses and thanked God for the custom-tinted windows on his BMW. He couldn't find Lara in the crew of people with ladders and paint buckets who swarmed the run-down clapboard home, and he knew he was well hidden inside his car. Turning right at the four-way stop, he considered going on home. This whole idea had *mistake* written all over it.

Melissa had phoned the night before, calling to ask if Jeremiah minded changing their lunch date from a tearoom to a small café across the street from her favorite antiques shop. She'd been hearing rumors that its chicken salad was to die for. As Jeremiah had watched Lara Crane's little car back out of his driveway, he heard himself telling Melissa that he needed to cancel their date entirely. Something had come up, he said.

Did it have to do with work? she had asked him. With architecture?

Rounding the block and starting down the street a second time, Jeremiah recalled answering in the affirmative. It was work. Architecture.

As the BMW again approached the old house, a man with a ladder over one shoulder turned to talk to someone on the sidewalk. The ladder swung sideways, just missing the car's tinted front window. Jeremiah stepped on the brake pedal, let out a breath...and there she stood. A halo of white paint spatters crowned the curly ponytail that topped her head. A brush in one hand. Freckles. She was chattering to the man with the ladder—her green eyes entirely too sparkly, in Jeremiah's opinion. He pulled over to the curb and got out.

"White paint?" he said. "Worst color you can put on a wall."

Lara focused on him and her eyes widened. "Jeremiah."

"Thought I'd drop by for some R & R."

"How did you find us?"

"Phone book." He hooked his thumbs in the back pockets of his jeans. "Someone's kid answered and gave me the address where you're working today."

"That would be my granddaughter." The ladder man held out a hand. "She lives with us. Might as well be ours. I'm Bill Scroggins. My wife and I founded Rehab & Renew."

"Pleased to meet you." He shook the man's hand. "I'm Jeremiah Maddox."

"The architect?" Scroggins's face sobered. "Listen, Mr. Maddox, this home is not for sale. Miss Ethel lives here, and we're making a few repairs for her. I read in the paper about you tearing down that old building a couple years back. R & R won't help you with that kind of thing. We do nothing but rehab."

"I came to help." He glanced at Lara. "To help her."

"Me? You did?" She swallowed. "But I'm... I thought tonight..."

He took a step backward. "Hey, if I'm not needed here—"

"Whoa now, buddy." Scroggins hand shot out and caught his arm. "We'll take all the help we can get. Lara, how about if you put him to work? I've got to climb up on the roof and check the flashing around that chimney. Miss Ethel says it's been leaking for years."

As the older man walked away, Lara pushed the sticky handle of the brush into Jeremiah's palm. "You can paint the trim in the living room. We don't have enough white for walls. We use goofed-up paint for those."

"Goofed-up?"

She headed for the house. "The paint stores sometimes mix colors wrong. Or a customer changes her mind and returns a few gallons. It's cheap, and no one minds a slightly oddball shade when they're getting a fresh coat on their walls."

"Who pays for all this? The flashing, the shingles, the paint?"

Lara swung around, green eyes suddenly narrowed. "Look, why are you here, Jeremiah? If you'd rather donate money, just make out a check to R & R. This work isn't about atonement. It's about giving. Don't do it unless you really want to."

"I'm here, aren't I?"

"You came because of what I said last night. I guilted you into it."

"I came for the blessing, Lara."

Her expression softened. "Then you need to meet Miss Ethel."

Jeremiah hesitated. He had come to be near Lara Crane. He spent the bulk of his time with developers, lawyers, draftsmen and designers. Teenagers took up what few hours remained in each day. Once in a while, he carved out time for something different.

As he climbed a set of rickety steps, ducked his head and entered a dimly lit room, Jeremiah felt a stab of doubt. Truth was, he didn't really want to meet Miss Ethel or anyone else on this street. He certainly didn't relish the idea of breathing paint fumes in this poorly ventilated house. He should have gone antiquing.

"Miss Ethel, this is Jeremiah Maddox," Lara said. "He's here to help."

"Well, bless my soul! Aren't you just the handsomest thing to come along for many a moon?"

Jeremiah peered down at a tiny, withered woman with sharp brown eyes and hands like bird claws. Toothless, she smiled up at him, and suddenly the image of Tobias Muraya flooded Jeremiah's heart.

"How do you do, Miss Ethel?" he asked, dropping to one knee and gently taking fingers knotted with rheumatoid arthritis. She was seated in a large, saggy chair with gold velvet upholstery worn away on the arms.

"I've been better, let me tell you." She spoke in a quavering voice and patted his hand as she talked. "I used to work for the telephone company, sweetheart. Back in the day, I was quite something. I could really get around—raised five children and buried two husbands. But I'm tired all the time now. My kidneys don't work right, and my ticker's nearly given out. I tell you what, sometimes it's all I can do to get myself out of bed in the morning. Would you like a cup of tea? Did you know you can make a box of twenty-five tea bags last for a month if you're willing to use them a couple times each? I don't mind sharing, not with a fellow as purty as you. Can you find the contraption that nice nurse brought over the other day for me...sort of a cane with legs?"

"Thanks, but I just ate breakfast, Miss Ethel," Jeremiah said, spotting the cane leaning against her chair. "Why don't you stay put, and I'll paint the crown molding and the baseboards for you. How about that?"

"What on earth is crown molding?" She smiled at him. "Well, you just do whatever you want, sweetie. You're so good-lookin' I could keel right over."

"Don't do that, Miss Ethel," Lara warned. She took an afghan knitted in orange, blue and black stripes and tucked it around the woman's lap. "We need you to stay warm and tell people what to do. Especially Jeremiah. He's clueless."

Giving him a wink, Lara turned and headed for the front door. "Enjoy the blessing," she said.

Jeremiah was about to tell her that he was hoping for a different kind of grace—the blessing of a woman with strawberry curls and green eyes and a voice that made his knees weak. But she was already out the door, letting the screen slam shut behind her.

"You ever had kidney trouble?" Miss Ethel asked as he dipped the brush into a can of white paint. "You know, we used to eat kidneys when I was a girl. My mama would kill a chicken and fry up the heart and liver—well, nearly all of it, to tell you the truth. Giblets, we called those leftover parts. I wonder if that's why I've had so much kidney and heart trouble. Payback, you know. From the chickens. Do you suppose that could be it?"

"Lunchtime," Lara sang out as she stepped back into the house. She half expected Jeremiah to have fled. Instead, he was down on his knees brushing glossy white paint onto the baseboards that rimmed Miss Ethel's living room.

"I went to work for the telephone company during the war," the old woman was saying. "My husband had been sent off to England. The European Theater of Operations, they called it. Left me at home with three babies and hardly enough to live on."

"That must have been rough." Jeremiah's eyes locked on Lara's face. "I asked Miss Ethel how she came to live in this house. She's been telling me the story."

"Ahh." Lara smiled. "You're up to World War Two. So, she's told you about the births of Reggie, Betty and Sue."

"We've gone back and forth a little. We began with the Depression. Then we traveled forward to the sixties when one of her sons got involved in drugs."

"Reggie," Miss Ethel spoke up. "That boy never was the same."

"How about a break?" Lara asked, sensing Jeremiah's need for a respite from Miss Ethel's warbling monologue. "It's noon. You can have half my sandwich, Jeremiah."

He stood and wiped his hands on his jeans, smearing white paint on the thighs. "I could run home—"

"I've got enough for two. Come sit on the porch. It's a beautiful day for late November."

As Miss Ethel began eating the lunch that Meals on Wheels had just delivered, Lara led Jeremiah out into the sunny afternoon. She had managed to stay away from him all morning, determined not to read more into his appearance at the site than she should. After all, the man had a busy career, active sons, new renters…and Melissa. Whoever she was.

They settled onto the porch, side by side, leaning against the clapboard wall of the old house. The rest of the crew had scattered nearby—some picnicking on a blanket in the yard, others resting in their cars. Lara handed Jeremiah half of her sandwich, poured him a cup of cold water and set a container of carrots between them.

"Did you see the Murayas this morning?" she asked, making conversation to keep her mind off the fact that his knee was two inches from hers.

"When I left the house, the two boys were playing with the dog out in the backyard. Have you seen the dent in the front of Peter's car? I'm surprised the thing even runs."

"That was his third car accident."

"You know every little detail about these people, don't you? How many times Peter Muraya has wrecked his car. The names of Miss Ethel's children."

She chuckled. "Why do you think my students call me the Grill Sergeant? I ask a lot of questions. So, tell me about you. Why did you really come here today?"

"About me. Forty-three, divorced, two sons, architect. Christian." He fell silent for a moment. "Not in that order…and I really came to see you."

She nearly choked on a carrot. "You didn't have to do that. We're having dinner tonight, aren't we? Or maybe you've changed your mind."

"I keep my promises." His blue eyes grazed her face. "I wanted to see you doing this…being yourself."

"I'm never anything but me. And listen, Jeremiah, you're a nice man. Nicer than I thought, actually. I don't want you to think I'm being standoffish, but I can't…I just really am not able to find a lot of time for people."

"Your whole life is about people."

"People like you." She covered her face with her hands and let out a groan of frustration. "You cannot have come here for *me,* okay? I'm not your type, and besides, I'm so far beyond all that. I'm thirty-five, and I have a doctorate and a good job. I was engaged for six years to the wrong man. I decided I really enjoyed working in Africa and helping international students and rehabbing houses more than anything. More than dating or whatever you want to call it. I'm single, okay? I go out with men sometimes, but I don't want to do the whole game. The serious stuff and the emotional roller coaster and all that. So don't be here for *me,* okay? Be here for Miss Ethel."

"Okay," he said.

Jeremiah munched on a carrot while Lara died of mortification, wishing she had kept her mouth shut and wondering why God hadn't given her a magic eraser to delete all the things she said and did that she wanted to take back.

"The front half of Miss Ethel's house is caving in," Jeremiah commented after a few minutes of awkward silence. "The leaking roof has rotted the frame. Patching the chimney isn't going to help. It needs major work— new trusses, drywall and insulation. Might as well redo the wiring and plumbing while we're at it. She's got a nice archway between the living and dining areas, but if she ever needs a wheelchair, she won't be able to get back to the bedroom or the bathroom. Those doorways need to be widened, and we'll want to put a ramp onto the porch."

Lara stared at him. "Jeremiah, R & R doesn't have the money or skill to do all that. We know how to paint and shingle and hammer a few nails. We can't rebuild the entire front of Miss Ethel's house. Most of us are weekend-handyman types. Amateurs."

"Well, you just got yourself a pro." He took a sip of water, crushed his paper cup and tossed it into the large commercial trash bin on the porch. "The boys and I will come over in the afternoons and on weekends. Let the others know in case anyone else wants to pitch in. Meanwhile, I'd better get back to Miss Ethel and her job at the telephone company." He stood and dusted sandwich crumbs from his paint-splattered jeans.

"Thanks, Jeremiah," Lara said.

He hunkered down and pointed a finger at her. "I'll help Miss Ethel," he said. "But I came for *you*."

Chapter Four

"Are you going to invite me in?" Jeremiah stood beside Lara on the front porch of her small bungalow. After working most of the day at Miss Ethel's house, they had gone out for curry at an Indian restaurant Lara liked. His stomach was full, his mouth pleasantly on fire and his arms aching to hold the woman who had amazed and intrigued him all day.

"No, you can't come in," she told him. "But thanks for the dinner. And I appreciate what you're doing for Miss Ethel."

"Why not? Ask me inside, I mean. I'm not the big bad wolf."

She smiled. "I think the gatekeeper at Oz said it best—nobody gets in to see the wizard. 'Not nobody, not nohow.' You may not be the big bad wolf, Jeremiah, but you're no Cowardly Lion, either."

"Well, I have the courage of my convictions. And if I want something, I'll try to get it."

"Is that so?" she asked. "I'm always looking for what *God* wants."

"Of course you are." He caught her hand as she reached for the doorknob. "Lara, I want to see you again. Today has been great, and—"

"Jeremiah, I already told you I'm not doing the whole dating thing. I made a lot of wrong choices in the past. I didn't like who I was or how I was behaving. But I'm on a new track now, and I plan to stay right here. You're not going to come into my house…or into my life. Ever. I don't need you, and I don't want you. Could I make myself any more clear?"

He lifted her hand to his mouth, blew a warm breath over it, and rubbed her fingers. "You're a cold woman. Cold hands. Cold heart."

"That's not true, and you know it."

"Shouldn't you ask what God wants you to do about me? I mean, let's be consistent here." He could read that his question had hit home. "Lara, have I asked for a serious commitment? I just want us to…well, to be friends."

"Friends?"

"Maybe more."

"No! I have a full, busy life, and I don't need that."

"I disagree." He took a step closer and saw the truth written plainly in her eyes. "You think you're fine all by yourself—just like I do. I've got my sons, my work, plenty to keep me occupied. I date on the fringes. Nothing serious."

"And what's wrong with that?" She tugged her hand from his and slipped it into the pocket of her coat. "I'm not lonely, if that's what you think. I'm comfortable being single. You and I had a pleasant evening, okay? Now would you just go away?"

He blew out a breath. "As I recall, the Wizard of Oz wasn't as fearsome as he wanted people to think. Even the Cowardly Lion got behind that curtain he used to protect himself. You may be able to do a few things that look a little like wizardly magic—wave your wand and find a home for the Muraya family or rehab Miss Ethel's old house. But inside, you're just a regular person."

Lowering her head, Lara was silent for a moment. "Good night, Jeremiah," she said. "I'll leave you a note the next time I check on the Murayas."

He watched her insert a key into the lock, turn the knob, open the door and step into the house. As she turned to shut him out, her eyes searched his face. Her voice was soft when she spoke. "Jeremiah, you're right. And I'm afraid."

The door closed, and he heard the dead bolt click into place. Standing on the porch, he wondered what he had hoped to accomplish by getting into her house…warming her heart…making her his friend, or more?

She was right to feel content in her role as a single person with an active life. For ten years, he had adopted exactly the same persona for himself. He had found great blessing in focusing on his sons and his career. Why should he expect Lara Crane to change? More important, why on earth would he want to bring any changes to his *own* carefully constructed world?

He didn't. Turning his back on her door, he walked to his car. He didn't want Lara any more than she wanted him. What had he been thinking?

* * *

Thanksgiving dinner at the International House on the campus of Reynolds University unfurled with all the flourish of a royal feast. Through her International Friends program, Lara had managed to connect every student with a local family for fellowship and cultural exchange. Some of the young people had been invited to their host's home for the traditional meal—but most were left to fend for themselves on this American family holiday. The I-House dinner filled the void.

"We have roasted a goat!" Peter Muraya entered the fellowship hall bearing a large platter covered with aluminum foil. His wife and baby followed close behind him, while Wisdom and Justice brought up the rear. "I think you will love this meat, Dr. Crane. All Kenyans eat roasted goat on special holidays. We dug a pit in the backyard in which to cook it."

Tabitha nodded with a warm smile. "The animal was procured for us by Jeremiah Maddox."

At the name of the man whose visage had filled her thoughts day and night for the past week, Lara suppressed a frown. She hated to think about the way she had spoken to Jeremiah on Saturday. Informing him that she had no interest in him. That she didn't even want his friendship. What kind of a Christian was she, anyway?

On the other hand, she couldn't have let him into her house. She didn't trust herself. He was too handsome. Too smart and interesting. Too much of everything she had always longed for in a man. If she had welcomed him into her life, she had no doubt what would have happened. The doors she had bolted shut would burst open, and the flood of desire she kept so carefully suppressed would wash over her in a drowning tide.

It wasn't physical desire that threatened her so much as the yearning for a deep, strong, lifelong commitment. She wanted a husband. A home. A family. Children. Since childhood, Lara had cherished the dream that she would become a wife and mother. It hadn't happened, and she had tried to convince herself she felt perfectly comfortable with the life God had given her. She did, too. Really.

But just the mention of Jeremiah's name brought it all back—that hammering in her heart. That need to be close to someone special. To belong. To love and be loved.

"The fat of the goat is the best part," Tabitha Muraya confided as she settled little Tobias into a high chair. "The men will eat it. They believe it makes them strong and brave."

Covering her mouth with her fingertips, she glanced at Lara and giggled. "In truth, it gives them a large stomach. Courage comes from the heart, does it not?"

Lara instantly thought of her flippant remark about the Cowardly Lion. "You're right, Tabitha, courage does come from the heart," she said. "We'll go ahead and let the men think whatever they want. Who likes goat fat anyway?"

She was helping Tabitha tuck blankets around Tobias when Wisdom tugged on her sleeve.

"Dr. Crane, we are going to Texas for Christmas," he announced. He stood like a little soldier beside his mother and the baby. Dressed in a freshly pressed white shirt and tan slacks, he looked every bit the handsome young gentleman. "We are going to drive in our car for many hours. My father's brother lives in Dallas. We will see their family—all our cousins! We will eat another goat and open gifts. It will be great fun."

"That sounds wonderful," Lara said, kneeling to meet Wisdom eye-to-eye. "I'll need to write down the dates of your trip so I won't come to check on you while you're gone. How is school these days?"

"My teacher gives me good marks. When I have trouble with reading or math, I tell Daniel. He explains everything to me."

"Daniel Maddox? He helps you with homework?"

"The young men and women come to the cottage nearly every afternoon," Tabitha said as she settled into a chair beside Tobias. The baby's eyes were drifting shut, and his head began to slowly tip to one side. "I am teaching them how to crochet. They want to make Christmas presents for their friends—scarves, you know? For the neck? All of the young people play with Wisdom and Justice. Even Tobias is very much loved."

Lara's eyes misted. "The teenagers are helping you."

"And the Murayas are helping *us*." Daniel Maddox's large sneakers appeared next to Wisdom's small brown tie-on shoes. "Hi, Dr. Crane. Dad said you invited us to the I-House for Thanksgiving dinner, so here we are."

Looking up, Lara focused on the tall, slender young man who had welcomed the Murayas into his family—and brought his father into her life.

Benjamin Maddox approached from the rear. "We have green bean casserole, Dr. Crane. The kind you make with cream of mushroom soup and fried onions. That's about as American as you can get."

"I made it," Daniel clarified. "All Ben did was sprinkle the onions on top."

"Welcome," Lara said, rising to greet them. "I'm glad you could come."

"We helped Peter kill the goat, too," Benjamin said, making a face as he drew a line across his throat with his index finger. "Not fun. But roasting it was cool. The smell of that smoke sticks to your body like a second skin."

"You can't wash it off," Daniel concurred. He spotted the oldest Muraya boy. "Yo, Wisdom! My man!"

Lara swallowed as she faced Benjamin. "So, your father is…?"

"Dad went to Bolivar. That's where my grandparents live." He swung away. "Justice, you rascal. Did you know your dog ate my shoe?"

"You left them outside," the small boy said. "That was unwise."

"They were muddy from playing football with you."

"Mdogo will always eat shoes if they are left outside. Even I know this." Justice's smile showed a missing front tooth. "Are you going to try that goat we roasted?"

"You bet I am," Benjamin said, laying his hand on the child's head. "Wouldn't miss it for the world."

Lara let out a breath as she turned to meet an Iranian student and his Pakistani roommate. Well, then, that was that. She wouldn't have to face Jeremiah after all. She had scared him off—which was exactly what she had intended. Now she could stop thinking about him and get back to her normal life.

As the cuckoo inside the Swiss clock in the hall sang out twelve noon, the students and their families began to gather around Lara. Campus rules prevented her from publicly blessing the food, but she was allowed to call for a moment in which everyone could silently offer prayers of thanksgiving. The moment she said, "Amen," a line began to form at the long buffet table.

Curry, rice, roasted goat, baked plantains, bean stew and dozens of other dishes sat steaming in long rows. Each offering was clearly marked with a small sign stating its country of origin and primary ingredients. Several of the students were Hindus and could not eat beef, while the Muslims could have nothing to do with pork. A few students were total vegetarians who didn't even eat eggs. With conversation flowing, laughter ringing out and exotic aromas mingling, Lara knew a surge of pure bliss.

This was what she was meant to do. This was who God intended her to be. Tears welled as she reached for a plate.

"Where shall we put the turkey?" Jeremiah Maddox stepped from behind her. With thick oven mitts protecting his hands, he carried a large roasting pan. A white-haired woman and a bald man appeared beside him, their arms filled with cardboard boxes laden with bowls of cranberry sauce, dishes of stuffing and baskets filled with hot rolls.

"There's room down here, Dad!" Daniel yelled from the far end of the buffet line. "You barely made it. What's the deal?"

"It's snowing!" Jeremiah called.

"Snow!" The word echoed across the hall like a hallelujah chorus. Suddenly the line to the buffet table evaporated as Nigerian, Saudi, Colombian and other students from all over the world raced to the door for their first look at the miracle.

"Snow!" someone shouted. "Yes, it is snow indeed!"

"Like sugar," one student cried.

"Soap flakes!"

"Salt!"

"Feathers!"

"Come, come. Let us go outside and see it!"

The mayhem gave Lara enough time to set down her plate and try to stop her hands from shaking. Why had he come? And those two people arranging the food must be his parents! Oh, this was not supposed to happen. And look how cute his mother was! And his dad...

Biting her lower lip, Lara focused on organizing the line that was beginning to form once again. The atmosphere at Reynolds created a sort of harmony that allowed students from hostile countries to gather in peace. But Lara was not naive. Trouble always simmered somewhere beneath the surface. She had to be careful who roomed together. She had to keep close tabs on every student—especially those from nations the United States did not consider allies. Even in the merging of a line at a buffet table, she knew tensions could mount.

As she helped the students gather in an orderly fashion, it occurred to Lara that if she could defuse potential conflict between nationalities, surely she could manage to get through this meal with Jeremiah Maddox in a civil manner. She would be polite, distant, kind but unemotional.

She filled her plate and took a chair near the student from Ivory Coast whose family was still missing. The young woman's eyes brimmed with misery. Friends gathered around her, and everyone began to eat. Lara noted that Jeremiah had joined his sons and the Murayas at a distant table, and she relaxed. Maybe she wouldn't have to summon any emotion toward Jeremiah. Clearly he had come to be with Peter's family, and that was exactly as it should be.

She had just taken a bite of Ethiopian injera, a spongy, sour flatbread used as a kind of edible table-cloth to soak stew juices and scoop up meat, when she saw Jeremiah's mother settle into a chair across the table. The woman's bright blue eyes matched her son's, but her face held none of his reserve as she pulled her napkin into her lap and looked around the table.

"I'm June Maddox," she said. "From Bolivar. That's about thirty minutes north of Springfield. My son is Jeremiah, over there with his Kenyan family. Are you young ladies from Kenya, too?"

"We are from Ivory Coast, Ghana and Cameroon," one of them responded in a low voice. "Our countries are in West Africa. Very far away from Kenya."

"My grandsons told me I'd learn a lot if I came to dinner here. To tell you the truth, I resisted the idea at first. We've always had Thanksgiving at home with Jeremiah and the boys. We have a daughter, too, but Jenny lives in California, and we don't see her very often. Oh, I'm telling you, we miss that girl! But she's like her big brother—busy, busy, busy. If Daniel hadn't met Peter and invited him to live in the guest cottage, I don't suppose Jeremiah would have ever slowed down. But he's a different boy since his African friends moved in. We haven't been introduced, but I believe you're Dr. Crane, aren't you?"

Lara swallowed a too-large mouthful of hot curry. "Uh, yes." She coughed and took a swig of water. "Your son has been very kind, Mrs. Maddox. Your grandsons…great kids."

"They all think so much of you. Especially Jeremiah. I don't believe he stopped talking about you during the whole drive down here from Bolivar. He says you run quite a program for these students. And you volunteer to refurbish old houses on the weekends."

"I enjoy my work."

"I can see why! This is just a delightful gathering. Wonderful." White hair freshly set and glowing with hair spray, she took a bite of turkey and chewed for a moment before speaking again. "I thought I'd start with a plate of my traditional cooking, you know. Then I believe I'll give some of the other dishes a try."

"I hope you will, Mrs. Maddox. The students have prepared the best their homelands have to offer."

"Jeremiah tells me his friends roasted a goat in his backyard. Actually, I'm not even sure that's legal."

"It's delicious, though," Lara said. Hoping to turn the conversation away from Jeremiah, she spoke to Dahlia, the young woman who had not heard from her family in several weeks. "Do you roast goats in an underground pit in Ivory Coast, Dahlia? I can't remember."

"Sometimes," the girl mumbled.

"I don't understand how it could cook very well," Mrs. Maddox spoke up. "Being buried like that. I thought fire needed oxygen to burn. Well, the main thing is that you have just won my son's heart, Dr. Crane. Or may I call you Lara?"

She wanted to shrink into her chair. "Lara, of course."

"Daniel and Benjamin were the first to tell us about you, and then Jeremiah started in. We had to hear all about moving the mattresses and the puppy and the painting project. You know, Jeremiah rarely mentions anyone except his business colleagues. But he has just talked himself half to death about you. Of course, I asked a lot of questions. The grandkids say I'm a busybody, but that's really not true. In fact, Jeremiah told me you like to ask questions, too, Lara. I think that's how to show you really care about someone."

"Yes, I believe it is." Lara searched frantically for anything to stem the tide of Mrs. Maddox's eager conversation. She focused on the students. "Perhaps some of you would like to share Christmas customs from your homelands. I'm sure our guest would enjoy that."

No sooner had Lara mentioned the coming holiday than Dahlia's face crumpled. The young woman was excusing herself from the table, tears streaming, when Mrs. Maddox caught her hand.

"My goodness, sweetheart, whatever is the matter?" Mrs. Maddox dug a tissue out of her purse. "Are you homesick? I bet all of you are! I hadn't thought about that, but you are a long way from your families, aren't you?"

"Dahlia cannot reach her parents by telephone or e-mail," one of the young women told Mrs. Maddox. "She is quite worried."

"Can't reach them?" The woman's blue eyes softened as she slipped her arm around the student.

"Well, I'm sure they're all right. Africa is such a long way from here, and you know how telephone cables break, and satellites go astray and things like that. I don't think you need to worry, honey. Here, take another tissue."

Lara watched as Mrs. Maddox slipped effortlessly into "mother" mode and took over the table exactly the way her son had taken over the Miss Ethel project. Within moments, the young African women were telling stories of their families at Christmastime, talking about boyfriends they had left behind, explaining political troubles and generally baring their hearts to the white-haired guest. Jeremiah's mother listened with great interest, her face registering shock or sadness or joy as each student spoke. With Mrs. Maddox's arm firmly around her shoulders, Dahlia stopped crying and even managed to eat a few bites from her plate. As conversation flowed, Lara took advantage of the opportunity to step away from the table.

Wandering from group to group around the room, she paused to thank people for bringing such wonderful food and for taking time to join their fellow students at the I-House. She glanced at the Murayas' table and noted that everyone was observing Tobias's first taste of applesauce.

This was working out exactly as it should, Lara realized. Never mind what Mrs. Maddox had said about her having won Jeremiah's heart. That was simply a figure of speech from a doting mother. Clearly the man was ignoring Lara, but she felt grateful that her words of rejection had not turned him away from the Muraya family or the tradition of the international Thanksgiving feast.

She took a clean plate and made her way to the dessert table, where confections of every kind were vanishing fast. Missing the traditions of her own parents who had retired in Arizona, Lara lifted a slice of Mrs. Maddox's pecan pie from its pan.

"Homemade crust," Jeremiah said, his chest brushing against the back of her shoulder and his breath warming her ear. "My grandma taught me how to roll it so thin you can almost see through it."

Her hand tightened on the plate. "*You* made the pie? That's a surprise."

"Didn't think I could cook?"

"Didn't think you had the time." She forced a polite smile on her face and took a sideways step along the table's edge.

He matched her, his long arm reaching toward a bowl of fresh fruit salad just as she touched the spoon. His hand closed over hers. "Pineapple this time of year?" he asked. "Wow. And what's that orange stuff?"

"Mango." She had no choice but to allow him to ladle some of the fruit salad onto her plate. "I think I can manage the spoon, Jeremiah. I've been feeding myself for years."

"Just thought I'd be of assistance. You're trembling so much you might spill something."

"If you weren't standing behind me…"

"If I weren't standing here, I wouldn't get to smell that perfume I noticed the other night and can't get out of my head. I told you I wanted to see you again, and here we are."

"You're with the Murayas, and I'm with the students. As it should be. Your mother is sweet."

"So is my dad. The boys are enjoying the work on Miss Ethel's house. Benjamin is crocheting a scarf for her."

"No way!"

He grinned. "It's your fault. Somehow you found a chink in my armor, and before I knew it my sons were crocheting, a dog was uprooting my two hundred tulip bulbs and a dead goat was roasting in my backyard. You, Lara Crane, are my undoing. And I'm planning to be yours."

"Good luck." She couldn't help but laugh at the images his words had evoked. "I don't have any chinks in my armor."

"Wanna bet?"

"Sure." Despite the knot in her stomach, she lifted her chin and cruised past him to refill her glass of punch. He followed and somehow reached the bowl ahead of her.

"How about dinner?" he asked. "Next Friday."

She tried to hold her glass steady as he filled it. "Busy," she said. "Busy, busy, busy. That's me."

"Saturday then. After we're done at Miss Ethel's, I'll pick you up for burgers and a milk shake."

"I'm busy from now until I turn ninety-nine. You can take me out on my ninety-ninth birthday. How's that?"

She glanced across the room to see people beginning to rise and clear the tables. Daniel was holding Tobias. Benjamin had crossed the room to introduce his grandfather to the students sitting with his grandmother. Dahlia was smiling.

"I can't wait until you're ninety-nine, and I won't." Jeremiah caught her arm as she tried to evade him. "I know the chink in your armor. You told me the last time we were together, Lara. You're lonely."

"I never said that."

"I heard it, though. Let's go out to dinner again and see what happens."

She faced him. "Jeremiah, I can't."

"Why not?"

"Who's Melissa?"

His expression sobered. "Melissa. How did you know about her?"

"Your cell phone. She called you. You said her name. Listen, I'm not some naive girl. I've been through all of this, and I won't do it again. Not the game. Not the flirting and playing around and seeing what happens. You won't have me on one evening and Melissa on the next. You won't have me at all, because I'm not available and neither are you."

"I ended my relationship with Melissa," he said. "That night when you heard us talking. I was supposed to spend Saturday with her, but I canceled so I could go paint Miss Ethel's baseboards. And see you. Best decision I ever made."

Lara stared down at her plate of pecan pie and fruit salad. Her glass of punch. Her plain shoes and black slacks and discount-store belt. This was not supposed to happen. She had worked too hard to make herself invisible, hiding behind her self-made curtain and performing wondrous deeds like the Wizard of Oz himself. How had this man found her? And what was she going to do about it?

"Yo, Dad." Daniel breezed up, Tobias in the crook of his arm. "Take the Tobester for me. Grandpa needs my help loading the car, and Tabitha is chasing down Wisdom and Justice."

He pushed the baby into his father's arms and dashed off. Tobias looked up at Jeremiah. Then he studied Lara for a moment. She wanted to sing with joy. Bending over, she kissed his fat little cheek.

"Bless you, Tobias," she said. "Keep Mr. Maddox busy, will you? He's way too nosy."

As if on cue, Tobias burped up a mouthful of applesauce. It spilled over Jeremiah's sleeve and onto the leg of his jeans. With an exclamation of dismay, he turned to look for a napkin. Lara whirled away with her dessert plate and found a cluster of tall Nigerians in which to hide.

Perhaps she did have a chink in her armor. Maybe she was a little lonely. Or a lot. But that one small opening didn't give Jeremiah Maddox license to come barging into her life. Certainly not.

Chapter Five

Jeremiah got the message. That didn't stop him from thinking about her day and night. He found Lara Crane's photo on the Reynolds University Web site. Beautiful. He programmed her number into his cell phone. At least fifteen times a day, he toyed with the idea of calling her. He tried to recall the smell of her perfume and the exact color of her eyes. Most of all, he pondered what it could be about himself that turned her away.

Since his divorce, Jeremiah had done his best to become a better man. But somehow he wasn't good enough for Lara. Was it the fact that he'd been married before? Was it his sons—both still living at home? Had she read those old newspaper articles that vilified his company, even though he was only the architect on the project and not the developer? Maybe she disliked his big house. Or his BMW.

As he drove to Miss Ethel's run-down home each afternoon at the end of a long day's work, he wondered if he was somehow physically unappealing to Lara. Too old? He checked his face in the rearview mirror for wrinkles. True, a few lines fanned out from his eyes. And he had noticed some silver hair filtering into the dark hair at his temples. Was that it?

Maybe it wasn't him at all. Maybe it was Lara. She said she'd been engaged to the wrong man for many years. Had made a mistake, chosen poorly. But so had Jeremiah. He had *married* his mistake. Committed himself to her before God. Had children with her. That was in the past, Jeremiah told himself. Why couldn't Lara let go of her own history? Sin and error didn't have to sit on a person's shoulders like those massive backpacks his sons toted to school and home again every day. Jeremiah had asked forgiveness of God, had been granted it, had moved forward.

Lara had told him to *get over it.* But had she worked her way out of her own guilt? To Jeremiah, she came across as a much better Christian than he. She had traveled further along in her faith and had learned to put her beliefs into action. Why couldn't she see that God could blot out her past and give her something— *someone*—new and better?

In a perpetual state of frustration, Jeremiah spent the weeks before Christmas driving from his home to his office to Miss Ethel's house and back home again. He missed Lara twice when she checked in on the Murayas, then left him curt little notes about how well the family was doing. She never mentioned her conversations with Jeremiah or indicated any personal interest in him whatsoever.

The woman was driving him crazy.

Snow fell, temperatures dropped and the boys brought the old Christmas decorations out of the storage shed. Benjamin was allergic to evergreen trees, so—as they did each year—the three men sorted artificial branches by their color-coded tags, inserted them into a green pole and gradually raised an approximation of a real tree from floor to ceiling. Jeremiah missed the fragrances of pine, fir and cedar that whispered "Christmas" to him from his childhood years, so he bought a couple of perfumed candles and lit them. It wasn't the same. In fact, nothing was the same as it had been.

These days more girls were hanging around the house along with the usual gang of guys. Jeremiah gave up trying to learn their names and sort them out. One evening all the young people gathered around the tree and hung balls, lights and silver swags while carols played on the stereo. The Muraya boys showed up to help decorate. Those two were always underfoot in his house, Jeremiah had noted—forever scampering here and there, giggling, running around with their socks hanging half off their little brown feet. Even the puppy began to call the Maddox home his own—sniffing boots by the door, nibbling popcorn and pizza crusts in the basement, chewing up one boot from a worn pair Jeremiah used for yard work.

A walk through the front door of his house no longer promised Jeremiah the serenity of stirring a pot of homemade chili in the kitchen, propping his feet by the fire and reading the newspaper while keeping an eye on the TV. Now he was met with balls of yarn, half-made scarves and crochet hooks scattered on every chair in the family room. Newspapers and magazines were dotted with muddy paw prints and marked with tiny holes from sharp puppy teeth. Small children chased each other back and forth in front of the television. The pizza delivery man stopped by two or three times a night, and Jeremiah wondered when he had lost complete control of his existence.

"Dad, hey." The younger of his two sons trotted up the basement steps as Jeremiah shut the front door behind him after work one evening in late December. Benjamin had his arm slung around the shoulders of a girl with long brown hair and big green eyes. She was too thin, Jeremiah thought, and she needed to hike those jeans a little higher around the waist. Who was this waiflike creature, and what had she been doing in the basement with his son?

"The Murayas are leaving for Texas tomorrow," Benjamin said, "and I was wondering if it would be okay to let them borrow one of our cars. Theirs is totally smashed in at the front, and it's always breaking down. What do you think? Maybe the BMW?"

"My car?" He gaped at the man-child staring him eye-to-eye. "That's the vehicle I drive to work. I'm not sending it off to Texas with five people and a dog."

"Yeah, but it's got four-wheel drive. You could use my car till they get back."

"Yours is filled with junk, and I have no idea when you last ran it through a car wash. No, Benjamin, forget it. We gave the Murayas a house. They can use their own car to get to Texas."

"But, Dad!" Benjamin followed his father toward the kitchen. "I'm willing to ride to school with Rachel these last couple of days. She says she'd be happy to take me."

Jeremiah paused and eyed the skinny girl. "You're Rachel?"

"Yes, sir." She looked scared. "I can drive Ben wherever."

"That's nice, but no one is giving up their vehicle. You have too many things going on before and after school, Benjamin, and so does Daniel. You can't expect Rachel to take you everywhere during the Christmas break. I need my car, too. Besides, I don't know if our insurance would even cover something like that."

"Dad, if I'm willing to let you use my car, then you should let the Murayas use yours."

"*Your* car?" Jeremiah raked his fingers through his hair. "Who owns your car, Ben?"

"Uh…you do."

"And who pays your insurance?"

"You. But, Dad—"

"No more!" Jeremiah exploded. "I've done enough for that woman! My house has turned into a three-ring circus, and I can't even find the hot chocolate these days. Nothing's where it's supposed to be—the whole place is a wreck. She asked me to help, and I did, and that's it. She's gotten all of me that she's getting. Ever!"

He turned and strode into the kitchen in search of something to eat. *Great.* The sink was full of dirty glasses and plates. A forgotten saucepan of soup had simmered on the stove until it was a gooey mass of noodles and burned vegetables. A ball of tangled red yarn lay in a heap near the pantry.

"Which woman?" Benjamin edged into the room, Rachel now behind him peering over his shoulder. "Are you talking about Dr. Crane?"

"No! Yes!" Jeremiah yanked on the dishwasher door and let it fall open, bouncing silverware in the plastic container. "When was the last time anyone ran this? Look at that sink! I had life running smoothly around here, and now look at what's happened."

"Dad, everyone knows you're just mad because you have a thing for Dr. Crane, so you should stop trying to blame her and just face reality."

"A *thing* for her?"

"You like her. You're nuts about her, and she won't give you the time of day, and you can't take it. And that's not anybody's fault but yours. You're all about being successful and getting what you want, but Dr. Crane isn't interested, because those things aren't important to her. She sees right through you. She knows you have to have your BMW and your fancy restaurants and your wool suits and silk ties. You're trying to show the world what a great person you are even though Mom left you. But nobody's interested in that anymore, Dad. Dr. Crane doesn't care, and neither do me and Daniel. We know we can't change what happened, so we're looking ahead to stuff we *can* do. Like helping the Murayas and Miss Ethel."

"What you *can* do is get your brother in here to clean this kitchen with you," Jeremiah growled. "And what you'd *better* do is stop judging how I choose to live my life and where I place my priorities. I'm helping the Murayas and Miss Ethel, too. I'm doing more than that, more than you or Lara Crane will ever know about. But that is *my* BMW out there in the garage, and I am not letting anyone take it to Texas or anywhere else. Is that clear?"

Benjamin glanced over his shoulder at Rachel, who shrank even farther behind him. "Yeah, it's clear, Dad," he said sullenly. Turning on his heel, he grabbed Rachel's hand and stalked toward the door. "Dan!" he yelled toward the basement door. "Get everyone up here! We've got to clean the kitchen for Scrooge!"

Jeremiah set his hands on his hips for a moment, surveyed the mess one last time and then headed for the back staircase to his bedroom. He could hear the pounding of feet racing up from the basement.

He paused for a moment before shouting, "And somebody better find my hot chocolate mix. Or else!"

Lara leaned her elbows on her desk and rubbed her temples. Thank goodness another semester was over. All her students had managed to pass their classes. All had found someplace warm and dry to spend the holidays. And surely *all* had visited her office at least once today to bid farewell. The place had been nuts.

She couldn't wait to get back to her house, run a tub full of hot water and sink down into a cushion of bubbles. Afterward, she would put on some Christmas music and phone her parents. Then she might order some Chinese food to be delivered while she decorated the plump little fir tree in the bay window of her living room.

As much as she enjoyed running the international program at Reynolds, Lara couldn't deny that it wore her out. If it wasn't a school-related problem, it was always *something*. For the umpteenth time that day, she lifted up a prayer of thanks that Dahlia's family had been found. Their situation in Ivory Coast was precarious at best, and they had gone into hiding—but at least they had reestablished contact with their daughter. Never had Lara seen anyone's face so filled with joy as Dahlia's when she burst into the office to announce that she had spoken with her mother.

Lara lifted her head and was reaching for her purse when once again the door swung wide and hit the back wall with a bang. Not again. This time it was Daniel Maddox. Breathing hard, he placed his palms flat on her desk, leaned over and announced, "Dr. Crane, we've got a problem. A big problem."

She forced down the surge of emotion that swelled inside her as she looked into blue eyes so much like his father's. "I checked on the Murayas two days ago," she told Daniel in a controlled voice. "They were expecting to leave for Texas this morning. Has something happened to their plans?"

"Yeah. You could say that. They left Tabitha and Tobias behind."

"What? That's impossible. Peter would never forget his wife and baby."

"He left her on purpose. Tabitha was feeling a little sick, so they decided Peter and the two boys would go to Texas without her and Tobias. But now she's getting *really* sick, and we haven't told Dad. We know we should, but he's been in a bad mood ever since Thanks-giving when you ignored him again. He's blaming you and us for everything, and he's had to drive up to St. Louis twice to check on his shoe factory condo project, which makes him that much more intense. The bottom line is that he's back home again, but me and Benjamin don't feel that great about telling him Tabitha and Tobias are still at the cottage and she's sick. So will you do it?"

Lara stood slowly. "I didn't ignore your father at Thanksgiving."

"Well, you're making him nuts, but that's not the point. Tabitha's running a fever. She called the house and talked to Ben about it. He asked me what we should do, and I decided to come see you, because Peter's your student."

"A fever?" Lara walked around the desk. "How high is it?"

"It was 102 this morning. Tabitha told Ben she was sweating a lot but she was shivering, too."

"Chills," Lara said, instantly concerned. "It could be the flu. A strain of it has been going around campus lately. Several of my students have had it. Has Tabitha phoned Peter to let him know she took a turn for the worse?"

"The Murayas don't have a cell phone. She can't talk to Peter until he gets all the way to his brother's house in Dallas. That won't be until tonight. Then he'll have to turn around and drive all the way back. Ben and me…we think you should come over and check on her."

"Has she taken any medication—like acetaminophen or ibuprofen—to try to bring the fever down?"

"I think she took something, but I'm not sure what it was. Dr. Crane, what about Tobias?"

At the thought of the brown-eyed baby, a pang of dread shot through Lara's chest. "Is he sick, too?"

"No, but Ben said that when Tabitha called, he could hear Tobias crying in the background. That's when I came to get you, and Ben headed over to the cottage to check on them."

Lara let out a breath. "You're doing great. Daniel, I appreciate your concern for Mrs. Muraya and Tobias. It's wonderful that you—"

"Just a sec." He whipped his phone out of his pocket and listened for a moment. "Yeah? Really? Did you tell Dad?" he rushed through the questions. "No, she's standing right here. Okay, okay."

He dropped the phone into his pocket and turned to Lara with an imploring look. "Dr. Crane, you have to come. Ben says the baby's crying, and Tabitha is feeling really bad."

Lara knew the circumstances must be frightening to the young men. If for a moment she believed Tabitha were dangerously ill, she would certainly step in, but Daniel seemed to be describing an illness that was at worst a case of the flu. Though she feared the Maddox family might interpret her resistance to help as indifference, Lara understood the importance of allowing them to work together at resolving this situation. Experience had taught her that when local families reached out to assist international students during difficult times, everyone benefited.

"Daniel," she said, "I want you to tell your father what's going on. He can help you and Ben handle this. I'm guessing that Tabitha has a touch of the flu. I know she freezes her extra milk, so Tobias won't go hungry. Thaw it in the microwave and make sure it's not too hot before you put it into his bottle."

"Aw, come on, Dr. Crane. We don't know how to do that kind of stuff. Please…you can't say no. They're your family."

"The Murayas are *your* family, Daniel. Go home and talk to your dad. I have every confidence that the three of you can handle it."

"Oh, great. This is just great." Daniel's face was pale. "He's gonna freak."

Lara rolled her eyes. "He'll adjust."

She picked up her purse and edged Daniel out into the hallway. He was still bemoaning his fate as she locked her office and led him down the steps and out the front door.

"You'll do fine, Daniel," she said. "I trust you."

As she walked toward her car, the snow that had been threatening all day suddenly came sifting down onto Lara's shoulders and nose. Puffy white flakes danced across the sidewalk, and she waved to Daniel, who had pulled up his jacket hood and was trudging toward home. It troubled her to entrust Tabitha Muraya and her baby to the Maddox clan. But if she did have the flu, no doubt she'd be feeling better by the next day.

Snow was falling fast as she negotiated the short drive to her house and pulled into the garage. Snowed in on a cold winter evening. Never mind about the Chinese food. An evening curled up on the couch in her pajamas, sipping hot apple cider and munching on popcorn might actually be enjoyable.

* * *

Lara lay basking in bubbles, adrift in the fragrance of jasmine and vanilla. She imagined her students scurrying away from school to begin the holiday season. Some would be a little sad. Others would rejoice. A few might sit alone, watching television and waiting for classes to start up again. But most would gather with friends and family, eat favorite foods, sing, laugh and return refreshed for the new semester.

No doubt the first day of school they would all want to drop by her office to regale her with their adventures, Lara realized. How many years had she been through this same routine? She began counting back, remembering faces and stories, getting sleepy and slightly chilled in the bubbly water…and then she became aware that someone was pounding on her door.

Instantly, she knew who it was. She gasped and sat up in the tub. What on earth could have happened? Was it Tabitha? Or Tobias?

The hammering intensified as she rose dripping from the water, grabbed a towel, patted her face dry and threw on a bathrobe. She was tying the belt as she stepped into her slippers and ran into the living room.

Peering through the small window in the door, she saw him standing on her porch. He wore a knitted cap and a navy down jacket, and his blue eyes stared back at her.

"What's going on, Jeremiah?" she asked as she pulled open the door. "Has something happened?"

Jeremiah stormed into the room and studied her for a moment. His stony face suddenly softened, registering a dawning surprise as he took in her chenille robe, her damp, pinned-up hair and her floppy pink slippers. "Were you in the bathtub?" he asked.

"Would you please tell me what you're doing here?"

"Tabitha's sick." He began to pace back and forth across the living room floor. "Very sick. We know it could be the flu—the boys both had that, and we rode it out. But the fever seems too high, and she's sweating and vomiting. Daniel looked up tropical diseases on his computer. There are dozens—Ebola, malaria, smallpox, dengue, yellow fever. The list goes on and on. She's too weak to tell us much of anything. I called the emergency room, and they said I should bring her in. So Daniel and I drove her through the snow. But Ben can't get Tobias to take his bottle, and neither can I. He's going crazy. Lara, I need you."

For a moment she could only stand and stare at him. Had he really said those words? This self-sufficient man who always got what he wanted…did he actually *need* her? She pushed her hands down into the pockets of her robe.

"What about taking the baby to the hospital?" she asked. "If a nursing mother isn't too sick, they—"

"No way." His eyes flashed with alarm. "Tabitha's practically delirious. The E.R. doctors wheeled her off right away. They said she might have something contagious. It might be some tropical disease. Can I bring Tobias over here?"

"To my house? But his crib and diapers are over there. The milk is in the Murayas' freezer." Lara's instinct to protect the baby battled with her certainty that Jeremiah could handle this.

"Look, you've raised two kids," she told him, her annoyance growing. "Surely you can manage a fussy baby for one night."

"No." His shoulders sagged and he rubbed the back of his neck. "I, uh…I didn't help much when Daniel and Benjamin were little. I was a lousy husband. A terrible dad. I didn't do my part with the boys, and I have no idea how to take care of Tobias."

"And you think I do?"

"Well…you're a woman."

"Unbelievable!" She threw up her hands and walked away from him. "I'm a woman so I'm automatically supposed to know how to take care of a baby, is that it? Well, I don't have children, and I don't have brothers and sisters, so I don't know a thing about it. I've been alone my whole life, and I intend to stay that way."

"Too bad!" he shot back at her. "You put the Murayas in my life, and now I'm in yours. You're not alone, Lara. You can't just go around doing good deeds and then sneak back to your little shell. You live in this world, and I'm a part of it, so you're stuck with me."

"Is this about you…or Tobias?"

"It's about *you.* Stop backing out and pushing away and running off. You are involved, and tonight we need you. All of us. Now, go put on some clothes and then get into my car, come over to my house and help me take care of the baby."

"Is that an order?"

"Yes, ma'am, it is."

"Fine. I can take orders. I can give them, too. Sit

down in that chair, and don't you dare move a muscle until I get back out here."

Helpless with frustration—and even worse, the knowledge that he was right about her—Lara stomped into the bedroom and slammed the door. As she tore off her robe and began to dress, she mentally admonished herself for giving in. And then she berated Jeremiah.

He was correct that she enjoyed retreating to her little house. Was that wrong? Jesus had taken breaks from healing, teaching and doing miracles to drift out to sea on a boat or slip up into the mountains to pray. Lara had the right to privacy.

She stepped into a pair of jeans and pulled them to her waist. None of the other families hammered on her door or barged into her house. Well...there was that time one of the international students had been caught shoplifting. And the day the INS threw three young men into jail for working more hours than their student visas allowed. Okay, and that evening a religious discussion in the student union building nearly erupted into all-out warfare. She had been called out of her home to deal with those crises. And a few others.

But she didn't want to go to Jeremiah's house. She didn't want to ride in his car or look into his blue eyes or listen to his voice. She didn't want to want what she wanted.

Simple as that.

Lara threw on a T-shirt and sweater, grabbed her coat and stepped back out into the living room. Jeremiah was talking on his phone.

"We're coming, we're coming," he said as he strode

back and forth across the wood floor. "Calm down. Feed it a banana. *Him.* Feed him a banana. Well, mash it up, Benjamin! You can do that much, for Pete's sake. And call Daniel to check on Tabitha. Yes, okay, we're on our way."

Lara pulled a cap down over her curls. "You got out of the chair," she said. "You failed to obey my orders."

He appeared confused for a moment, then he gave a sheepish grin. "Your tree. It's real. I had to get up and smell it."

Lara glanced across the room at the small Christmas fir. Boxes of decorations sat around it, ready for the evening of tree trimming, popcorn and hot cider she had planned. But she noted that the glistening angel she always put at the top was already perched in place, gazing down at her and Jeremiah with a beatific smile.

Chapter Six

Jeremiah opened the front door of his house and stepped into the foyer as Daniel and Benjamin crowded in behind him to get out of the cold. After dropping Lara off at his house earlier that night, Jeremiah and Benjamin had driven back to the hospital to check on Tabitha. During their journey, the snow had turned into rain, and the rain into ice. With temperatures rising and falling, the roads treacherous and people already overdoing the Christmas holiday, the hospital had maximum traffic. Tabitha had been transferred to an isolation ward, but getting information about her condition had proved to be a nightmare.

"You guys hit the hay," Jeremiah told his sons. "Daniel, you're going over to work on Miss Ethel's house in the morning, right? Benjamin, you've still got school. I'll check on Tobias."

"And Dr. Crane." Benjamin gave his father a sly smile. "It's okay, Dad. We know how you feel about her. It's fine with me and Daniel."

"Daniel and me," Jeremiah corrected as he shrugged out of his coat. "And you don't know a thing about it. Dr. Crane is here because she runs the international student program. She's helping us out until Peter gets home. I wonder if he's made it to Dallas yet. Did Tabitha give you that phone number?"

Both boys shook their heads. Well, they would visit Tabitha at the hospital again in the morning and get the information from her then. The main thing now was to make sure Lara had been able to cope with the baby while the men were away. Jeremiah would take a quick look at his answering machine, grab a granola bar from the pantry and head over to the cottage to check on them.

As Daniel and Benjamin started up the stairs to their rooms, Jeremiah pulled off his cap. A shower of water droplets scattered across the marble floor. He hung the cap on a hook in the foyer's closet and stepped into the living room.

The sight that met his eyes nearly took his breath away. In a rocking chair beside the fire, Lara cradled the sleeping baby. Red-gold curls tumbled around her face while her green eyes gazed at him, and for a moment he imagined himself transported into a Renaissance portrait of the Madonna and her Holy Child. A soft, maternal glow radiated from the woman's face. Her blue sweater and jeans blurred into a formless shape around the baby wrapped in his white blanket. The only thing missing was the lowing of cattle and the choir of angels.

"How is Tabitha?" Lara asked him in a low voice.

"Not well." He walked silently across the carpet toward her, the spell not quite broken. "The doctors don't know what's wrong yet. They're trying to get in touch with a tropical disease specialist. Infectious disease."

"Don't worry. Tabitha's been in the States nearly a year and has given birth to a son. If she had brought something contagious from Africa, we would have known before now."

He bent over and looked down into the folds of the velvety blanket. Tobias drifted in sleep, his eyes closed and his lips plump and pink. Lara rocked back and forth, holding him tightly.

"I found Tabitha's milk in the freezer," she whispered. "She had stockpiled quite a bit. It should get us through tomorrow. The cottage was cold, so I gathered some supplies and brought Tobias back over here."

"Sure, that's great. What about the crib?"

"I'll hold him."

"All night?" He pulled up a chair and sat down across from Lara. "You need your sleep."

"I can sleep here. I had dozed off before you came home." Her eyes deepened. "How sick is she, Jeremiah? Tell me the truth."

"It's worse than any flu I've ever seen. She was shivering and sweating. She kept calling out for Peter. No matter how many times I told her he was in Dallas, she couldn't get it through her head. She cried a lot about Tobias, and she kept saying things in Swahili."

"Poor Tabitha. We've got to get her family back here. I'll talk to the president of Reynolds tomorrow. Somehow we'll figure out a way. The college has benefactors and special funds. We can fly the Murayas home if we have to."

They sat in silence, comfortable together for the first time. Jeremiah leaned back in the chair and watched the glowing blaze cast a flicker of shadows on Lara's face. She stared at the flames.

"What's the weather like?" she murmured.

"Frightful," he said. "The fire, however, is definitely delightful."

She smiled. "Well, I guess we have no choice but to let it snow."

"Actually, it's been raining. And freezing."

"Uh-oh. I was planning to go Christmas shopping."

"I'm afraid you're stuck," Jeremiah chuckled. "My house is yours."

She glanced at him a moment, then turned away quickly. Again they lapsed into a quiet peace. Jeremiah tried to recall the last time he had felt so warm, so relaxed, so perfectly at home in his own house. There were no teenagers running up and down the stairs. No pizza delivery men ringing the doorbell. No cell phones warbling or televisions blaring. It was just Lara and the baby. And him.

"I'm sorry," he told her. "About tonight—banging on your door and ordering you around. And before—not wanting to take in the Murayas. After making so many mistakes in my early adulthood, I've tried to be a good father. A good man. But I'm probably pretty much the same guy I always was."

"Actually, you've changed a lot. You're very different from the man I met a few weeks ago."

He looked at her in surprise. "How?"

"You have an African family living on your property.

You roasted a goat in your backyard. You ate Thanksgiving dinner at the I-House and brought your parents. You're repairing Miss Ethel's home. And now you're sitting beside a fire with Tobias and me."

"That last part is my favorite."

She shifted in the chair. "The important thing is that you're open. You've reached out to people. And you've let people in."

"What about you?"

"I've always reached out."

"Not to me. You won't touch me, and you won't let me near. Your walls are so high I don't stand a chance of getting over."

"You don't have to. I'm already inside. See? Here I am in your living room."

He shook his head. "You did everything in your power to keep from coming over here to help the boys and me."

"I have to maintain a professional distance. I can't get too involved personally with my students."

"I'm not your student, Lara. Why won't you get involved with me?"

She swallowed. "Why would you want me to? Jeremiah, you can have anyone. Melissa or whoever you choose. I'm not available."

Once again, he knew a sickening thud in the pit of his stomach. "It's because I'm divorced, isn't it? I have too much baggage. The boys, the years alone, the failed marriage."

"We both have baggage. I just don't think yours matches mine. I spent six years wearing the engagement ring of a man who didn't have time for me. It was long ago, but it's still very real. He worked for the famine relief agency that had hired me, and we met in France. He was with the home office. He trotted around the globe, stopping now and then to remind me that I was in love with him. Then away he went again. Alone, I earned my doctorate and started working at Reynolds, and then suddenly one day I woke up. I realized he wasn't ever going to make a life with me, and that was okay. I didn't want to be married. I hated having my emotions jerked around and played with. I despised wondering about him and fretting about the future and always feeling like something was missing. It just wasn't worth it, you know?"

Jeremiah sighed. "Sure I know—I *was* that guy. Overcommitted to my work and undercommitted to my family. Gone all the time. Selfish to the core."

He reached out and took her free hand. For a moment, he held it, stroking down the length of her fingers one by one. "Lara, I'm trying very hard not to be him anymore. And I think you really don't want to be the un-attached, unemotional, uninvolved woman he turned you into. When I look in your eyes…when I watch you with Miss Ethel…or my boys…I see the tender woman inside. You hold Tobias, and…and I believe you wish you could turn back time as much as I do."

The baby whimpered and she drew her hand away to tuck in his blankets. "We can't turn back time, Jeremiah. I'm who I am."

"I like who you are. You're beautiful. Smart. Gifted. Kind. Generous."

"Stop." She blew out a breath. Tobias squirmed, and

she lifted him to her shoulder and began to pat his bottom. "Is this what you say to women? Don't say it to me. Don't play with me. Words like that are scary, Jeremiah. They're disturbing. They make me feel…"

"Feel what?"

"Oh, I don't know!" She stood, and with the sudden movement, the baby began to cry. "I've put that part of me away. That swooning, romantic, idealistic girl. The hope and the desire. Imagining how it could be and wanting it. No—I'm not doing that anymore."

"I wasn't lying when I said what I think of you, Lara," he said, standing and walking beside her as she paced the floor and jiggled Tobias up and down. "I meant every word. I feel different about you than I've felt about any other woman. It's because *you're* different."

"No, no, no. It's just the weather and the baby and all the changes. You're off-kilter. Give it time, and you'll be back to normal."

"I don't want to go back—ever." He tried to get her to look at him, but she had turned her face away as the baby's sobs increased in intensity. "I like listening to Miss Ethel talk about the Depression and the war and the telephone company. I loved roasting that goat with the Murayas. You brought me those things, Lara. Why won't you let me near you?"

"Here. Here, take this baby." She held Tobias out, and now Jeremiah saw that her cheeks were streaked with tears. "Take him and give him some milk. I'm going home."

"Don't go, Lara. Please. Just talk to me."

He tried to maneuver the wailing little boy as he

followed Lara into the foyer. Fists clenched and head bobbing, Tobias cut loose with a screech that could wake the dead. Jeremiah struggled to control him and try to prevent Lara from putting on her coat. It was impossible. As the baby wailed, she tugged her hat over her curls.

"The milk is in the freezer," she said, sniffling. "And don't do this to me ever again, Jeremiah Maddox."

With that, she pulled open the door and stepped outside. Jeremiah had no choice but to hurry toward the kitchen, baby in arms, praying he could remember how to work the defroster on the microwave.

Where were the bottles? How hot should the milk be? Did people sterilize things these days? He pulled open the freezer door and spotted the small white bags Lara had brought over from the guest cottage. Grabbing one, he tried to make soothing noises while he opened the microwave door.

"It's okay, Tobias," he murmured. "Don't cry. I've got you, buddy. I'll have this milk ready in just a second, and you're gonna be feeling a lot better before you know it. If I could just…set you down for…"

"Give him to me."

Jeremiah turned to find Lara standing in the kitchen with her arms out. "You brought me over here. I don't have my car. And besides, the roads are covered with ice."

He straightened, digested the information and grinned. Well, well, well.

Lara slept in a recliner with Tobias in her arms until she woke to find him a soggy bundle, still blissfully lost in dreamland. Jeremiah had been right—he didn't know a *thing* about babies. At least she'd had some experience with children through her work with the famine relief agency and the families in the international program. Somehow she and Jeremiah had managed to warm the milk, pour it into a bottle and get Tobias to drink from something that was most definitely not his mother. They had changed his diaper and found him a clean dry blanket.

It had been well after midnight when the baby fell asleep again and Lara sank exhausted into the recliner. Though she had told Jeremiah to go upstairs and get a good night's sleep, he refused. So they drifted off together in separate chairs, in stocking feet, with the fire warming their toes.

The sound of a footfall on the staircase brought Lara awake, but Jeremiah slept on. She studied the man beside her, his dark hair and lashes, the planes of his face softened and relaxed. Recalling what he had said the night before, Lara wondered if he really meant those words. *Beautiful. Smart. Gifted. Kind. Generous.* Did he see her that way, when she had come to think of herself as plain, stoic, evenhanded and professional?

She could hear someone in the kitchen, and she suspected it was Benjamin, preparing his breakfast before heading off to school. What would he think if he knew what his father had said the night before to the director of Reynolds University's International Student Program? Had Jeremiah considered his sons at all when he spoke so openly to her? *You won't touch me, and you won't let me near. Your walls are so high I don't stand a chance of getting over,* he had said. Did he even think about how his two boys might feel if their father breached Lara's walls?

Studying Jeremiah again, she listened to his deep, slow breathing. Her heart swelled as she permitted herself to imagine that picture she had dreamed of once, long ago. A man and a woman, united, married, in love. A home. A fire. A family. Arms to hold her in the night, hands to wipe away her tears, ears to listen to her hopes and fears and sorrows.

"Dad! Hey, Dad! Did you hear the news?" The voice grew louder, and then Benjamin was standing in the living room staring at the two adults. He halted, took in the scene, assessed it.

Jeremiah blinked and squinted against the morning light. "Huh? What's going on?"

"They canceled school." Benjamin stepped closer. "I ate breakfast and made my lunch and got my backpack ready. Then I looked outside and saw the ice. So I turned on the radio, and every school is closed for the day. I figured you were probably…you're usually up before me but… Uh, hello, Dr. Crane…how's the baby?"

Jeremiah leaned forward until the recliner's leg rest folded in. He rubbed his face with both hands for a moment. Then he smiled at Lara.

"Dr. Crane and I were up late feeding Tobias and changing his diaper," he told his son. "Then the roads iced over. So here we are."

Benjamin eyed her. Then he nodded. "Okay. Listen, I'm heading back to bed, Dad. I don't think you should go to your office. The weatherman said this is the worst ice storm to hit Missouri in years. Maybe ever. Whole trees are cracking in half. Branches have fallen all over the streets. The snowplows can't even get out."

"Then I'll stay home," Jeremiah said.

"Really? You never stay home." Again Benjamin looked at Lara.

Uncomfortable, she concentrated on the baby, who was stirring now and beginning to fuss. If he were a good father, Jeremiah couldn't ignore his sons. Benjamin would want an explanation, and Daniel would demand it. Surely it wasn't every morning they awoke to find a woman sleeping beside their dad—double recliners or not.

"I guess we'll be here together today," Jeremiah said. "All five of us."

"Four," Lara corrected. "I have to get home. I need to call the hospital and find out about Tabitha's condition and get the number where Peter and the boys are staying. Then I've got to contact the president of the university and see if we can pull together the funds to bring the family back together."

"Dr. Crane, you can't go anywhere today," Benjamin told her. "You're stuck with us."

"And we have telephones at our house, too." Jeremiah handed her a cell phone.

"I can walk home," she protested. "I need clean clothes, and there's probably not enough food—"

Jeremiah cut her off by holding up one hand. "We've got plenty to eat. With teenagers in the house, we stay well stocked. We could make it through a nuclear winter, let alone an ice storm."

Lara could see she wasn't making headway. "I need to not be here," she said finally. "Just not *here*."

With that, Tobias let out a wail and there was nothing to do but focus on the baby. "I'll teach you three wise guys how to do milk, diapers and mashed bananas," she said over the din. "Then I'm walking home. Here, Ben, you get the first round of Tobias duty."

Lara held out the squirming tot.

Benjamin backed up. "I'm not changing his diapers."

"Come on, big guy. He won't bite."

"You stink," Benjamin told Tobias as he lifted the baby into his arms. "If you think I'm looking at what you deposited in your diaper, fella, you're wrong."

Feeling as if she had been pounded with a large hammer, Lara edged forward to climb out of her recliner. Before she could get up, Jeremiah pressed the footrest in and took her hands to help her. She stood, realized he was much too close and tried to move away. Impossible. He reached out and brushed a curl from her cheek.

"She looks beautiful in the morning, doesn't she, Ben?" he asked.

Benjamin glanced at them and grinned. "Yeah. No getting around that, Dr. Crane. My dad has a good eye when it comes to women."

"I'm not one of your father's women," Lara said, pushing past Jeremiah. "I'm here in an official capacity, as a representative of the university. And I hope you have orange juice. I always start the day with a full glass. Now, let's get some milk down that baby. Wow, what a pair of lungs."

She hurried toward the kitchen, praying neither man could read her face. She didn't want to be just another woman in Jeremiah Maddox's life. If she ever dared to let a man into her heart again, she intended to be the *only* woman. The difficult night had made her grumpy, and she ached for a hot shower, a change of clothes and a long nap.

But Tobias wasn't about to let anyone forget him. He bellowed with rage, his single white tooth gleaming in his open mouth. As Lara took a bag of milk from the freezer, Daniel emerged from the hallway into the kitchen.

He scowled. "What's all the racket? Dr. Crane, is that you? What's that smell?"

"Your turn to change his diaper," Benjamin said, pushing Tobias into his older brother's arms. "Dr. Crane is teaching me how to heat the milk."

"I'm not changing anybody's diaper." Daniel turned to his father. "You do it, Dad. And why is everyone at home? I thought you had school, Ben."

"Canceled. I bet we'll be out tomorrow, too, and that's the last day before Christmas break. It's pure ice outside."

As if to emphasize his point, a loud cracking sound reverberated through the house. Everyone turned to the window just in time to see an enormous limb fall from the oak tree in the backyard. Daniel handed Tobias to his father and the two boys raced to the back door. Jeremiah held up the howling baby.

"Young Mr. Muraya, why do I always get stuck with you?" he asked. "Every time I'm anywhere near, someone dumps you into my arms. Well, come on, kiddo. Let's get you cleaned up."

Lara smiled tiredly as she set the microwave to heat the milk. Everything inside her screamed along with Tobias—let me go, get me home, somebody help me! But at the same time, she couldn't deny the pleasure of padding around a warm kitchen floor in her stocking feet, pouring herself and Jeremiah glasses of orange juice and listening to the two boys exclaim over the crystalline wonderland that was their yard.

"There. Done," Jeremiah said. Lara watched him lift the baby into his arms as she approached. He took the bottle and tipped it up for Tobias. "See, I can be taught, Dr. Crane. Can you?"

"What do I have to learn? I'm the one who figured out the milk and diapers."

He glanced at his sons, then he leaned close to Lara's ear. "You have to learn how to let me in."

"Nobody gets in to see the wizard," she murmured back.

"You're wrong. I'm coming in."

"Don't even try."

"I'm already halfway there."

Lara focused on his mouth, so close to her own. Diapers and popping tree limbs and the taste of orange juice on her tongue vanished in an instant. Yes, he was. Halfway there, she thought. And if she wasn't careful, every reason to keep him out would evaporate. Then he would be all the way in, and her heart would hurt, and her mind would get tangled and all the things she didn't want would come roaring back.

No getting around it, Lara was stuck. One step out onto the front porch of the Maddox house, and her feet nearly shot out from under her. Jeremiah would not be driving her home, she realized, and she certainly would not be walking.

Jeremiah sat in the recliner with a peaceful Tobias in his arms as he listened to the weather reporter drone on with bad news. Lara keyed the number of the hospital into her cell phone. The storm hadn't been confined to Springfield. As it turned out, ice coated every highway, street and road in a perfect arc that swung downward from Missouri through northern Arkansas and eastern Oklahoma and ended just south of Dallas, Texas. Snow blanketed the states to the north and rain fell in the south. But in exactly the worst possible place, temperatures continued to plummet, and the ice settled in for a visit.

"I need to speak to a patient by the name of Tabitha Muraya," Lara said when someone picked up at the hospital. The phone had rung a long time before anyone answered, and then the breathless receptionist told her that very few workers had been able to make it in that morning. The whole place was understaffed, people who had tried to walk to their cars or drive the icy streets to work were pouring into the E.R. and everything was a mess.

All the same, in moments Lara was connected to the unit where Tabitha was being kept in isolation. "Are you a member of the immediate family?" the nurse asked briskly.

"No, I'm—"

"I'm sorry but government regulations prevent me from giving out any information about our patients. You'll have to contact a family member, ma'am."

"I'm caring for the only immediate family member in Springfield," Lara said. "I have Mrs. Muraya's five-month-old baby. I'm not able to reach her husband, because he went to Texas. I need to speak to Tabitha."

"That's not possible, ma'am. I'm sorry."

"Can you give her a message?"

"Umm…I can give it to her, but I can't promise a response."

"Okay." Lara flashed Jeremiah a look of frustration. "Tell her that Mr. Maddox needs the telephone number where her husband is staying in Texas. We need it as soon as possible, so we can tell him about the situation and get him back here."

"I'll do what I can."

Jeremiah held out his hand. "Mind if I intervene?" he asked Lara.

She gave him the phone.

"Yes, ma'am, this is Jeremiah Maddox," he told the nurse. "Yes, *that* Jeremiah Maddox. I'm on the hospital's board of directors, and we've got a very difficult situation here. As you know, the board places top priority on doing what's best for the patient. May I speak to someone in administration please?"

Lara gaped as he continued talking. *The board of directors?* All her life, she had placed money and power at the bottom of the list of admirable qualities for a man. Rock bottom. Jeremiah had both, and she hadn't trusted him for a second. His big house, fancy car and eye for women had relegated him instantly to her dishonor roll of scumbags. Only his genuinely wonderful sons, his efforts to accept change and his determination to help Miss Ethel had edged Jeremiah out of the muck. She had begun to like him. Admire him. Even respect him.

But she had still held his wealth and position against

him. Now, he spoke on the phone, gently but firmly using his place on the hospital board to come to the aid of the Muraya family. And for the first time in her life, Lara began to appreciate the value of influence.

Sinking into the recliner beside Jeremiah, she observed him as he went about the business of manipulation. It was a fascinating process. A person had to own a profitable enterprise in order to make money, Lara acknowledged. Money had led Jeremiah to a valuable social position on the hospital board. A feather in his cap. A vanity role for a wealthy man—unless it could be put to use. Position brought power, Lara realized, and power wielded by a godly man could be a good thing. A very good thing.

Before Lara had time to fully absorb this revelation, Jeremiah was speaking to the president of the hospital. It was a complicated situation, he reiterated. A baby was involved. No immediate family in the state.

"So exactly how serious is Tabitha Muraya's medical condition?" Jeremiah asked. Leaning back in the recliner, he flipped up the footrest. "I see. Well, that's a concern. No, the baby is going to be fine—don't worry about that. I've got that under control. Absolutely. Thank you, then. We'll be in touch."

He set the phone on a nearby table and looked at Lara. "Malaria," he said.

Chapter Seven

"Malaria is the wrong diagnosis," Daniel announced as he stepped into the living room. He pulled a chair up to the fire where Jeremiah and Lara had set up camp for the day.

Setting a sheaf of papers on his knees, he began to explain. "The doctor said Tabitha was having a relapse of malaria, right? So, I did some research. There are three kinds of malaria in Africa. *Plasmodium falciparum* produces severe symptoms and is responsible for most malaria deaths. *Plasmodium malariae* causes typical symptoms, but it can remain in the bloodstream for years without producing symptoms. Neither one relapses."

Jeremiah studied Lara for a moment. She was feeding Tobias again. To everyone's consternation, the baby had turned out to have a voracious appetite. They were down to the last couple of bags of their frozen milk supply, and no one knew what to do next. Only a few streets had been cleared, the weather reporters were warning people to stay home, and nightfall was closing in.

Jeremiah focused on his son again. "The doctor definitely told me Tabitha's having a relapse, Daniel. What's the third kind of malaria?"

"*Plasmodium ovale.* It can relapse, but it's found in West Africa. The fourth strain is only in Asia." Daniel tapped on the paper. "Tabitha is from East Africa. She can't have *P. ovale,* and she can't have the Asian strain. So this is not a malarial relapse, Dad. I think you should call the hospital and tell them."

"Who am I to tell an infectious diseases specialist that he's wrong? This doctor must have information we don't."

"Got something new!" Benjamin crowed as he hurried into the room with paper in his hand. "I've got you beat, Dan-the-Man. In Africa, malarial relapse is seen exclusively in *P. ovale,* and represents a reseeding of the bloodstream by dormant parasites in the liver."

"That's exactly what I just said," Daniel protested. "It's in West Africa, and Tabitha is from East Africa."

"Aha, but that's a *relapse.* As it turns out *Plasmodium malariae* can recrudesce!"

"Recrudesce?" Lara frowned. "What on earth does that mean?"

"The malaria can renew or become active again. *Plasmodium malariae* can continue to cause clinical malarial attacks even twenty years after the original infection. And get this. There's now drug-resistant malaria all over Africa."

"Let me see that," Daniel demanded. He snatched Benjamin's research.

Jeremiah rolled his eyes. Nothing worse than the younger brother trumping the older. In the recliner beside him, Lara looked as though she were about to fall asleep with Tobias in her arms. The preceding hours had been long and stressful for everyone—including the baby, who was clearly feeling the absence of his mother and family.

With a great deal of effort and a lot of string pulling, Jeremiah had managed to establish contact with the doctor treating Tabitha. The man was less than optimistic. Her fever continued to spike, and she had been very nauseous. He had diagnosed her with a relapse of malaria and was treating her with chloroquine.

At midmorning, Daniel and Benjamin braved the ice and gingerly made several trips to the guest cottage. They brought the crib and carrier over to the main house, along with every diaper, wipe, lotion and jar of baby food they could find. They also located an address book, which turned out to have many wrong numbers, erasures and illegible names.

Typical of an international family in transition, Lara had explained. Finally, in the late afternoon, she got through to Peter. Deeply upset on learning of his wife's condition, he decided to set off immediately on the long drive home.

A few hours later, Peter had called the Maddox house to say that his car had broken down several miles north of Dallas. He and his boys were back at his brother's house, and there was no telling when they would be able to repair the car, let alone drive it back to Springfield.

Jeremiah blamed himself. If he had listened to his son, he would have loaned Peter the BMW. So what if the kids played in the backseat and the dog chewed a hole in the upholstery? It would have been better than this predicament.

Lara's call to the president of Reynolds University went unanswered. He must have left town for the Christmas holiday. Her hope of finding funds to pay for the Murayas to fly home went down the drain. Feeling guilty and wanting to do more to help, Jeremiah offered to take care of the tickets himself. He had enough frequent flyer miles for all three Murayas, and he could send a cab to pick them up at the house where they were staying.

That hope was dashed when word came that the Springfield airport had shut down and few flights were arriving at or leaving DFW. So, they were stuck with a hungry baby, a desperately ill Tabitha, and no Peter, Wisdom or Justice. Jeremiah could only pray for a heaping helping of heavenly mercy.

"Did you say the doctor is treating Tabitha with chloroquine?" Daniel asked. "The new malaria is resistant to that drug."

Benjamin stood to challenge him. "She's got the old malaria. It's just recrudescing."

"I'm gonna recrudesce *you!*" Daniel started for his brother. "How much you wanna bet he's treating her with the wrong drug?"

"Two large pizzas and a movie!"

Benjamin neatly evaded his brother's lunge, and both boys raced out of the room, their feet pounding on the wooden staircase as they went back up to continue their investigations.

"Sometimes I think they're still a couple of kids," Jeremiah said.

"They are. Smart ones." Lara repositioned the sleeping baby. "They may be on to something. I've heard about drug-resistant malaria. I hope the doctor knows what he's doing."

"What are *we* doing, Lara?"

"I don't know about you, but I'm thinking about those last two bags of milk and a long night ahead. Do you suppose one of us should venture out to the store for some formula? I need to get home anyway, and if you could drive me there—"

"Don't go." The words were out before he could think.

She looked at him in surprise. "Jeremiah, I haven't changed clothes for two days. I'm a mess, and I'm worried that my water pipes may have frozen. Besides, I need a shower and a good night's sleep."

"Stay here. With us." He turned to the fire, fumbling to find the right way to tell her what was in his heart. "Lara, I'll take care of you. I'll go out and buy the formula, a toothbrush for you, new clothes, whatever you need. Just stay here."

"But you and the boys are managing Tobias very well."

"It's not about the baby. It's Christmas."

"Jeremiah, I'm not some present Santa dropped down your chimney."

"No, you're a gift from God." He met her green eyes. "You've changed my life, Lara. If you hadn't come along, I would have kept going the same way forever. Just doing the basic requirements. Taking care of the boys and myself. Never stepping outside my boundaries. I'm so grateful for what you've done for us. For me."

She fell silent for a moment. "You've done things for me, too. But, Jeremiah, I don't exactly like them. You shouldn't ask me to stay here. You can't expect me to be a part of your family at Christmas. I have another life."

"What are you so afraid of, Lara?" Leaning forward, he took her hand. "What is the problem? Do you dislike me?"

"I like you, okay?" Her eyes flashed. "I like the boys. I like everything here. But I don't want this…the havoc inside me. It's your fault. You keep saying things…and touching me." She drew her hand from his. "I'm too mature and stable for all this. What it comes down to is, I don't want to deal with a bunch of chaotic feelings."

She pushed herself up from the chair. "The temperature is falling. You'd better go get the formula before the streets get really treacherous. Tobias is awake. I'll change his diaper and play with him for a while. We'll put off feeding him as long as possible, and then when you get back, we can try the formula. I don't know if he'll take it, but we can see."

Jeremiah stood. "Why wouldn't he drink formula?"

"Because he's used to his mother's milk," she said, a note of sudden desperation in her voice. "He's accustomed to life the way it always was. He won't want anything different or new. He might be frightened. You can't expect someone to change just like that, don't you see?"

"Lara." He stepped to her and slipped his hands

around her shoulders. "Lara, don't be afraid of me. I won't hurt you."

"What if I hurt you? Have you thought of that? I might walk out on you the way your wife did. I might be just like her."

"You're nothing like her."

"You should be skeptical of me, Jeremiah. That would be prudent."

"You stayed engaged for six years. You don't walk out on people, Lara. You told me that, and I believe it."

She looked up at him, her eyes brimming. "I don't want to go anywhere near that memory. Please. Doubt me the way I doubt you. And let me go."

"I can't." He pulled her into his arms, drawing her as close as he could with a chunky, wiggling baby between them. "Lara, I've thought it through. Life is short, and God brought you into mine when it was almost too late. Please stay."

He bent his head and kissed her lips as tears spilled down her cheeks. "Jeremiah, oh, this is not good," she breathed. But even as she spoke the words, she moved against him, lifting her chin and seeking his kiss.

"Give me one more day," he said. "If you still feel the same tomorrow, then go home."

"I *am* going home tomorrow—no matter what."

"Maybe the ice will stay and keep you here." He kissed her again, drinking in the sweetness of her lips and the warmth of her skin against his. "Maybe we can freeze time. Freeze everything. Leave it this way forever."

At the sound of male feet pounding down the staircase, he drew back. She hung in the moment, her eyes closed and her lips moist. And then the boys burst into the room.

"Hey, Dad, Dad!" Benjamin cried out. "Three of the guys are out driving around in their cars, and they said the streets aren't too bad yet. They want to bring some of the girls over here. What do you think? We could all keep an eye on the Tobester."

Daniel nodded. "And they'll bring pizzas and chicken and whatever we want."

"Yeah, we need to finish our crocheting, Dad. Everybody's yarn and hooks are over here, and those are our Christmas presents. Please!"

"What about school tomorrow?"

"Canceled!" Benjamin high-fived his brother. "It's Christmas!"

Jeremiah forced himself to face the pair of hooligans in his living room. Where had these aberrations of nature come from? Why was their hair so long? Why did their shoes always smell so bad? And how could they be so blind as to miss the fact that their father was falling in love?

He looked at the woman across from him. Then he focused on the pair of bright brown eyes between them. At least one person in the room hadn't missed a thing.

Lara and Jeremiah stayed up most of the night keeping a watchful eye on the throng of young people who were crocheting, laughing, eating popcorn and pizza and watching movies. She ferried empty pizza boxes to the upstairs trash. He toted sodas to the basement. And in between, they struggled to manage a baby boy who definitely did *not* like store-bought formula.

Tobias, as everyone discovered, had the healthiest lungs in the neighborhood. His array of vocal emanations ranged from whimpering to sobbing to wailing to all-out screaming. The kids in the basement took turns walking him around, up and down the various staircases in the Maddox house. But to no avail. Tobias had evidently decided he'd had enough.

Jeremiah thought jiggling perhaps might ease his misery. This resulted in the last of the good milk erupting from the baby's mouth and spilling down the master of the house's back. Lara—so exhausted she felt half-delirious—could hardly keep from dissolving into maniacal laughter.

She tried one way after another to get Tobias to drink formula. He spat it out. He let it dribble from the side of his mouth. He shook his head with such vigor that the liquid sprayed the kitchen wall from ceiling to floor.

And the later the hour, the louder the baby. At one point in the night, someone suggested taking him to the hospital to see his mother. But a rushed call to the ward resulted in the information that even though Tabitha's condition was improving, Tobias was absolutely not allowed on the floor.

Countless diaper changes and repeated efforts to feed, rock, walk and otherwise comfort the baby had little effect.

As the sun rose over the icy wonderland outside the Maddox house, Tobias suddenly went silent in Lara's arms. She called Jeremiah to her side and they stared down at the baby in alarm. Tobias looked at the two of them for more than a minute without blinking. Then, as if abruptly resigned to his destiny, he shut his eyes and fell sound asleep.

Lara drifted off in the recliner beside the fire, and Jeremiah sprawled on a couch nearby. Their respite wasn't long. Cell phones began ringing, kids came tromping up the stairs, car engines roared to life in the driveway. Word came that the airports in Springfield and Dallas were both open, and the Murayas had found a flight home. Eventually, Jeremiah and his sons left the house for the short drive to the Springfield airport.

Tobias woke up, decided formula tasted pretty good after all, and was happily having his lunch when his father and two brothers walked in the front door of the Maddox house at noon on the day before Christmas Eve. Lara could have wept for joy.

"What is this news they tell me about you, Tobias?" Peter exclaimed, lifting the baby from Lara's arms. "Are you making trouble, my son?"

"He's finally decided to accept baby formula," she told him.

"Formula? What about rice cereal? Bananas? Pudding? This boy loves to eat."

Lara looked at Jeremiah. In their frantic efforts to get Tobias to take the formula, they had forgotten all about the jars of pureed food that Daniel and Benjamin had brought over from the cottage. She let out a breath.

"I told you I knew nothing about babies," she said.

Jeremiah chuckled. "Chalk it up to experience."

"But he is healthy," Peter said with satisfaction. "He is alive and well—what more can one ask? Take your brother, Wisdom. See if you and Justice can make this stubborn child smile."

"If you don't mind leaving your boys here with my sons, I'll drive you over to the hospital," Jeremiah told Peter. "I'm sure Tabitha is worried about everyone."

"And you can drop me at home on the way," Lara put in.

Jeremiah grimaced. Since their conversation beside the fire, Lara had done everything possible to avoid another private moment with him. It hadn't been difficult.

As everyone regrouped and began to don coats, hats and gloves, Jeremiah took Lara's arm. "Thank you," he said. "Thanks for helping us."

She tried to smile even though her heart was breaking. "Just take me home, Jeremiah," she told him in a low voice. "I need to be where I belong."

The ice storm was losing its grip on southern Missouri, Lara noted as Jeremiah's car inched along in traffic. Trees had split in half. Huge branches and thick limbs lay scattered across yards and on roofs. In several places, power lines had gone down. But Springfield was beginning to bustle again as last-minute Christmas shoppers braved the streets to run their errands.

The car pulled into Lara's driveway, and she reached for the handle. Jeremiah caught her hand. "I'll call you," he said.

"I can find out about Tabitha by phoning the hospital," she replied. "Jeremiah, don't call."

Before he could respond, she stepped out of the car and picked her way across the yard to her front door.

Chapter Eight

Jeremiah didn't call, and Lara was grateful. She told herself it was for the best. Each of them had a full, happy life. Why complicate it? In short order, he would find another woman—or return to Melissa perhaps. And Lara might call the economics professor who had been pestering her for nearly a year. She didn't mind the occasional date. Someone uncomplicated and easy.

She stretched out on her sofa and let her focus blur until the lights on her Christmas tree went soft and luminous. The trouble with Jeremiah was that he had never been simple. He was too handsome, for one thing. Too sincere. Too great a father to his sons. Too successful in business. Definitely too rich.

Most of all, he had been far too serious. Every time he had looked at her, she heard unspoken messages zipping back and forth between them. When he touched her hand, she could have sworn she already knew the warm pressure of his fingers and the flat plane of his palm. Worst of all, his kiss had evoked swirls of emotion and vibrant colors of hope and joy that raced through her like a drug. She had wanted more. More of him. And that frightened her beyond belief.

Christmas Eve. She had called to wish her parents joy, and then she had driven to her church for the annual candlelight service. After that, she picked up a Chinese dinner from one of the many take-out restaurants that dotted Springfield. Finally at home again, she ate and listened to music and tried very, very hard not to think about Jeremiah Maddox.

Tucking a quilt around her feet, Lara pondered the Muraya family. Earlier in the day, a hospital receptionist had informed her that Tabitha had gone home at last. Tobias must have been greatly relieved to see his mother again, Lara thought. What a crazy couple of days those had been.

She shut her eyes and was recalling that Daniel owed Benjamin two large pizzas and a movie…when someone knocked softly on her door. Without thinking, she instantly imagined Jeremiah standing on her porch, and she leaped up from the couch and threw open the door.

And she was right.

"Merry Christmas," he said as snowflakes swirled through the night air around him.

She took his arm and pulled him in out of the cold. And before she could properly digest the fact that he had come or what she should do about it, she was wrapping her arms around him and laying her head on his shoulder.

"Jeremiah," she murmured. "Oh, I missed you. I don't know what's wrong with me, but I've missed you every minute of every hour of every day since you dropped me off. I thought I would never see you again, and I told myself that was fine, but I didn't feel it. I wanted to see you so much and…and please make me stop blabbering before I embarrass myself any more."

He laughed, tipped up her chin and kissed her lips. "How's that?"

"Better." She closed her eyes as he folded her close against his chest.

"Lara, did you think I was going to let you get away? Didn't I tell you from the very beginning what I wanted?"

"But I'm so afr—"

"Don't say it." He put his finger on her mouth. "Don't ever say that again. Lara, both of us can dig up plenty of reasons to run from each other. How about if we don't?"

She nodded. "I'll try."

He set her away from him and eased her down onto the couch. "My greatest fear was loving a woman who couldn't commit. Then God brought you into my life— a woman deeply committed to everything and everyone."

"Oh, Jeremiah."

"Your greatest fear was having to play the game— the drawn-out dance of dating and the emotional roller coaster. So, I've decided to dispense with all that."

As she looked up at him in confusion, Jeremiah dropped to one knee. "Lara Crane, I love you. Will you marry me? Tomorrow?"

"Tomorrow's Christmas," she managed.

"That's right, and I have your gift." From his pocket, he drew out a small black box. Was that a diamond sparkling inside it? She couldn't see clearly through her tears. She blinked as he slipped a ring onto her finger. "Merry Christmas, my love."

She brushed her cheek. "You want to marry me?"

"As soon as possible."

"Yes," she said, throwing her arms around his neck. "Oh, yes, Jeremiah. I love you so much."

The black box tumbled to the floor, but neither one noticed.

There were certain advantages to wealth and power, Lara had discovered. Hospitals could be manipulated. Airplane tickets obtained. And weddings. Weddings could actually be performed on Christmas Day.

Lara wasn't quite sure how it all came about, but somehow hundreds of red roses filled the small alumni chapel at Reynolds University. Clusters of happy people from Namibia and Indonesia and Brazil and China crowded into the pews. An elderly couple from Bolivar showed up to witness the marriage of their son. And another delighted pair arrived from Phoenix in time to see their daughter marry a fine, handsome gentleman.

As she walked down the aisle of the chapel, her white gown trailing through a sea of rose petals behind her, Lara focused on the man she loved.

No six-year engagement. No endless emotional merry-go-round. He had given her this gift.

Together, hand in hand, they vowed before God to have and to hold each other. This day. And forever.

As the organist played a final hymn, Jeremiah kissed Lara. It was the happiest moment of her life. So she kissed him back. And then he kissed her again.

"Dad! Hey, Dad!" Benjamin bounced into view. "The photographer is waiting, Dad. We've gotta get the pictures taken, because everyone's coming over to the house."

"Miss Ethel will be there and Benjamin crocheted her a scarf," Daniel said. He took his father's arm and turned him away from Lara. Facing them both toward the photographer, he instructed, "Smile, Dad. Smile, Dr. Crane."

"We should call her Lara," Benjamin interjected. "Or how about Mom?"

"We'll figure it out," Daniel informed his brother. "Later."

As flashbulbs popped and countless people kissed Lara on the cheek, she clung to Jeremiah's arm. She could not have asked for anything more. Not one single thing…except…

"Just a minute," she said, lifting her skirts and stepping down from the altar. She crossed the rose-strewn carpet to the Muraya family.

"Excuse me, please," she said, reaching down to the pew where a still-weak Tabitha sat. "May I borrow this?"

As Jeremiah grinned, she returned to his side. "Take a picture now, please," she told the photographer.

Between them, Lara and Jeremiah balanced the contented brown-eyed baby. As the flashbulbs went off, Lara bent and kissed his small chocolate cheek.

"Merry Christmas, Tobias," she whispered.

Jeremiah murmured in accord. "And thank you from the bottom of my heart."

CHRISTMAS, DON'T BE LATE

Jillian Hart

The Lord appeared to us in the past, saying:
I have loved you with an everlasting love;
I have drawn you with loving-kindness.
                    —*Jeremiah* 31:3

Chapter One

Amanda Richards had learned that hope was like a credit card. If you used it too much, you went over the limit and, *voilà,* no more charging. No more hope.

Yep, that's me, she thought. Totally maxed out on hope and in need of a bucketload.

What was she going to do now? She swiped the snowflakes from her lashes and tried not to let the freezing winds trouble her. She studied the long steeply rising hill above the broken-down car—the road home. The veiled Montana Rockies and silent snow-covered forests surrounded her, but no help of any kind. No driveways, no houses. Nothing.

She thought of her two little ones in the backseat, growing colder as each second passed. She bit her bottom lip to keep the frustration inside. Apparently luck was like hope, and she'd used up her limit on both.

Don't die on me now, car. She gave a helpless look at her car's engine compartment. The raised hood blocked some of the snowfall as she bent over the radiator cap. The Trusty Rusty, as she called the four-door thirty-year-old sedan, had seen her Aunt Vi through twenty years, two cousins through lean college years, and now it was hers.

The price had been right—free. But then, she'd had to pay to have it towed to the nearest mechanic. Not the best deal on the planet, but since Todd had taken off for parts unknown with their five-year-old minivan, leaving behind a divorce decree and more medical debts than she knew what to do with, she'd take whatever gifts the angels sent her way. And, until this moment, this gift had been the utmost in dependability.

Okay, Trusty Rusty, let's get you running. If that's possible. Amanda gripped the sizzling hot radiator cap one more time.

Please, angels, let it be possible. She thought of her little girl bundled up in the backseat, so desperately ill. This cold would not be good for her.

The scorching burn of metal went right through her insulated gloves while she twisted the stubborn little cap. Hot, hot, hot, her brain told her, but she ignored it. Come on, just a little more. She could feel the cap give, but it was like grabbing a fistful of fire. Pain over-whelmed her and she let go.

The cap now sat in cockeyed defiance, firmly stuck on the radiator. Amanda didn't even mutter in frustra-tion, as she heard the telltale sound of a car's side window, loose in its frame, being unrolled. She ripped off her glove and, dropping to her knees, plunged her hand into the snow berm made by the last snowplow to have braved the windy and narrow country road.

She might be out of hope, but she was not out of fortitude. She would let both her blistered fingers and the stubborn radiator cap cool a bit more and she'd try it again.

"Jessie's gettin' cold, Mom."

She turned at the sound of her son's voice. Jeremy had popped halfway out of the window, twisting his torso so he could keep an eye on her. His blond hair stuck up in unruly shocks and the worry in his brown eyes made him look far too old for his age.

Her heart warmed at the sight of her precious firstborn and she forgot all about her scorched fingertips and the wet snow seeping through the knees of her jeans. He was a seven-year-old blessing and challenge all at once. Too smart for his own good, too cute for hers. "Roll the window back up so you don't let in more cold air. I'll have this figured out in a jiffy. Don't worry, okay?"

"She's real cold." He gave his electric-blue muffler a swing with one free hand and watched the fringed ends dangle into the snow.

"It's not safe to hang out the window, you know that."

"Yeah, but I *could* hang out the *other* window on the other side. That'd be worse. A truck would come along and—" He balanced on the edge of the door and clapped his hands together. "Hey, you know what? I'm gonna go home an' get the sled an' come back with the barbecue. Then I could make a fire and you an' Jessie could get warm."

"Leave it to you to find the perfect solution. But sadly,

your little sister and I will be icicles before you get back.
Now sit down, buckle up and close the window."

"Na-huh! I could fly there like Wonder Boy. He's my
favorite superhero next to Jesus."

"Jesus isn't a superhero, honey."

"I know that! He's the *greatest* hero."

It was hard to argue with that. And since they could
use a hero about now, she sent up a prayer, not for
herself but for her kids. *Just a little help, Lord, please.
Just enough to get us by. That's all.*

Surely that wasn't too much to ask.

But as if in answer, the brush of snowflakes against
her cheek was sharp-edged and icy. When she tilted her
head back to look up at the gray, heartless sky, she
feared her prayer hadn't risen on wings but had fallen
to the ground right along with the snow.

Since her hand wasn't stinging so much, she pulled
it out of the berm. She didn't care about the pain or the
blisters. What she cared about was getting the kids
home. At least it wasn't too far, considering. She laid
her hand at her throat. Although she could not feel the
plain gold cross through the layers of winter clothes,
she felt better just knowing it was there. Her mother's
cross. Her mom had been a true believer, unwavering
in her faith.

It wasn't that she didn't believe, Amanda thought,
it was that she just couldn't see. She'd been walking
by faith and not by sight for so long, she didn't know
where she was anymore. She was running low on
faith, too.

Well, it wasn't as if they could just sit here. The winds

swirled, as if promising a blizzard soon. There was no way she could let her children—especially poor Jessie— be caught in that. And until they were out of the dead zone, she couldn't call her aunt for help on her cell phone.

A little help, Lord. Please. She yanked on her glove. When she tried the cap again, it was much cooler but still hot enough to burn while she worked the stubborn thing off.

The radiator was bone-dry, just as she suspected. She stared at the empty compartment and felt the last vestiges of courage slide off her like the snow on her coat.

Yep, it looked as though she was all out of luck. And radiator fluid.

She closed the hood with a slam. Through the melting globs of snow on the windshield, the children were watching her. Jessie was standing on the backseat in order to see better, her eyes too big for her peaked little face. Jeremy had pulled himself up like a little soldier at roll call.

I can't let them worry. They have enough on their plates right now. It was her job to handle the worries and hardships. It was theirs to be kids.

She checked for traffic before she stepped out onto the road, an automatic response from living in Portland, even though it was so quiet that she could hear a vehicle coming from half a mile away.

She slogged through the deep snow unflinchingly, for she was still a Montana girl down deep at heart, and opened the back passenger door. "All right, ten hut. We're going to take a scenic hike. Jessie, baby, let's get your hood tied up tight."

Her sweet little girl stared up at her with troubled blue eyes, and her Cupid's mouth scrunched into a heartbreaking frown. "I don't wanna."

"I know, but it will make you like a bunny."

The little girl's frown didn't lessen, although she nodded grudgingly. It had been a hard morning for her, being poked and prodded at the hospital.

Amanda brushed aside silken red curls before she tied the fuzzy hat's strings into a bow beneath Jessie's little chin and tried with all her self-discipline to hold back the tide of anxiety within her. Then she tugged the thick parka's hood over the top. "There, now you can pretend you have beautiful long bunny ears. Jeremy, zip your coat all the way, honey."

"Then I can't fly, Mom. I'm Wonder Boy."

"Even Wonder Boy zips his coat when it's snowing." She snagged the old stadium blanket the kids used in the car from the floor where it had fallen and wrapped Jessie up in it for added protection.

"That's because he keeps his identity secret," Jeremy explained as he hopped off the edge of the backseat and into the snow. "That way he can go around helping people and no one knows who he is. It's real important to help people."

"You're right. Now help me out by grabbing my bag and shutting the door, please."

"Okay!" He hurried to comply.

"I'm cold, Mommy." Jessie hiccuped.

"I know, baby. Snuggle close, okay?" Amanda held her little one tight. Her spirit swelled with love for her baby, but sometimes love wasn't enough. She'd give her life for her daughter's in a snap, but she'd already tried that bargain with God. To no avail.

"Here, Mom!" Jeremy jumped at her side, holding out her heavy bag, stuffed full.

It weighed a ton as she slung it onto her shoulder, taking care not to jostle her ill little girl.

The wind blew harder as they started out. She kept her steps short to accommodate Jeremy and took his hand. The feel of his fingers wrapping tight around hers, holding on with so much need and confidence, humbled her.

So much was riding on her decisions. On her strength. On her frailties. The only thing she knew for sure was that she would not fail her kids.

She twisted just enough to take the brunt of the vicious wind and shelter Jessie from the snow. It was falling harder now, pinging through the air like thousands of icy miniature bullets and it thickened like a veil falling closed, until the tall jagged Rockies disappeared and all that remained of the endless forest were dark shadows just out of reach and just out of sight.

The world felt so far away. Maybe that was a good thing, since that meant the hospital was far away, too. If she concentrated hard enough, maybe she could push this morning's visit out of her mind and the anxiety of waiting for the results of Jessie's tests.

But no, nothing could diminish the icy fear taking root in her soul that this new medication had had little effect. Nothing could lessen the fear that this could be Jessie's last Christmas.

And if that came true, then her strength of will

could not change it. All the love in her heart could not change it. She was out of luck and out of prayer. All out of everything.

Snow battered her but she kept going, hoping against hope that the promise was true.

That she really wasn't walking alone.

Colton Nichols pulled his truck to a halt in the middle of the snowy country drive. The only traffic was a parked car hugging the berm. The two shadowy figures climbing the hill looked like a young mother and her kid, struggling in the deep snow.

If he were back home in L.A., he'd wonder if he was being set up for a possible carjacking. Okay, so he'd gotten a little cynical. This was Montana. He was in a no-crime zone, so he stopped, zipped the power window down and leaned across the seat. Felt a jolt of surprise when he realized the young woman was carrying a smaller child, wrapped well against the cold.

She was hooded in a bulky navy parka, her face half-covered in an ice-caked scarf, her intelligent eyes considering him carefully. Those eyes were all he could see of her, as blue as a lake in winter right after a thaw. Clear and deep and true.

His heart quaked to life, as if for the first time. Funny, it'd never done that before. "That's a load of responsibility you have there. You might as well get in. I'll take you where you need to go."

"Thank you so much for stopping." The woman lifted the child she carried into the warmth first, protecting her from the cruel wind with her body. "Our car conked out.

We're in the dead spot where there's no reception, of course. That makes you a lifesaver."

"Nope. Just a neighbor. You need help here?"

"We're fine now. My little one can't be out long in the cold."

It was strange how the wolf's howl of the wind, the beat of the icy snow on the glass and roof, the whir of the defroster and the *swipe, swipe* of the wipers faded into stillness. Dimly he was aware of the kid heaving open the back door and clambering onto the back bench seat.

He was captivated, that was the word. Utterly mesmerized. He couldn't say why. Maybe it was her calm gentleness as she settled the little girl onto her lap, or the love in her big blue eyes as she brushed a few lingering snowflakes clinging to the preschooler's fine curls, peeking out from beneath her furry hood.

"Is this a real monster truck?" asked the kid in the back.

"Not even close."

"It's *like* a monster truck. You should get those big knobby wheels. Then you could crunch up a big hill and fly up over the top."

"I'd need more than a monster truck to fly. I'd need to get my cape back from the dry cleaner's and a team of reindeer from the Northern tundra." What a funny kid. Colt put the truck in gear, easing slowly on the gas. He wasn't much of a snow driver, but the tires dug in and the truck crept forward. Dizzying snow gusted against the windshield, cutting visibility. "It's getting worse. Looks like I came along just in time."

"It's a blessing—that's what you are. Every time I'm looking doom in the face, it's as if the Lord is letting me know I'm not totally facing complete and utter devastation."

He liked the way she said that with a smile. "I'm not what you'd call blessing material. Too much of a cynic. My name's Colt."

"I'm Amanda Richards. This cutie here is Jessie." The little girl didn't even look as if the cold had affected her, she'd been wrapped so well. So lovingly. Cozy on her mom's lap, she studied him over the tight wrap of her pink muffler, covering half her cherub's face. "Jeremy's the superhero in the back."

"That's me!"

Colt studied the kid's reflection in the rearview mirror. "It's been a long time since I've seen a superhero."

The boy wiggled in excitement in the backseat. He'd tugged off the red-and-black cap he'd been wearing beneath his coat's hood, and he'd unzipped the plain parka jacket so that his red sweatshirt, with the big gold letters NDER BO, showed as he reached forward to aim the heater's vent directly on him.

That sure took him back. Colton hated to count the years to know how far. "Wonder Boy used to be my favorite crime fighter, too."

"He's way cool!"

Amanda rolled her eyes. "Hey, Wonder Boy, sit back on the seat. Belt yourself in. You know these things."

"Yeah, yeah." Good-naturedly, Jeremy slunk back and grappled with the belt.

The poor man. She cast a sideways glance at Colt behind the wheel. He wasn't wearing a wedding ring. The last thing he probably felt comfortable with was a mom and two kids fogging up his truck and dripping melting snow on his leather seats.

He didn't seem too upset, not judging by the way the corners of his mouth stretched into an amused grin. He was a good-looking, big guy. It looked as if he spent a lot of time in one of those expensive gyms. And everything about him shouted "top of the line."

Okay, so she was feeling a little shabby. It wasn't as if she were interested in dating him—or any man—heaven knew that was the last thing she wanted or needed. But she was still a woman. She tried to ignore her faint reflection in the polished windshield—her hair was windblown and straggly, emphasizing the dark pockets beneath her eyes big enough to store change in.

She looked like a woman down on her luck, scraping by and going without sleep to watch over her terminally ill child at night. The small wave of vanity slid away and she pressed a kiss to her baby's temple. *Please, God, let things stay just this way. Make time stand still.*

Impossible, she knew, but a girl could ask, right?

"I've seen your truck on the road. I figured you had to be the new neighbor. Rumor has it that the O'Ryans sold to a guy from California."

"I know what you Montanans think of guys from L.A. You think I'm citified."

"Sadly, but at least you've got the right vehicle to fit in. A Montana Cadillac."

"That's what the salesman called this rig, too." He grinned, friendly and easily, showing even white teeth and kindness in his black, fathomless eyes.

She felt a flash of light roll through her, as if light-

ning had forked down from heaven and buzzed her side
of the truck. But no thunder followed. As if blinded by
a sudden brightness, the colors around her faded away,
the howl of the wind, the hum of the engine and the fan
from the defroster silenced. Her heartbeat slowed, as if
time stilled.

It lasted only for a second. Then the brightness
vanished, her pulse double beat and there was Colt, unaffected, steering the rig onto the shoulder, to avoid the
SUV barreling down the middle of the narrow country
road at them.

Whatever that was, it was proof she was way too
sleep deprived. She gave Jessie another snuggle. Not
that she minded the long nights watching over her baby.

"That was close." Colt shook his head. "Guess they
own the road."

"They probably do. I take it you haven't met the
Cowins?"

"I haven't met anyone yet. Only my second day here."

"But rumor has it that you bought the house
sometime in the summer."

"August. Been busy working. Where do I let you off
at?"

"You know the first mailbox you come to along this
road, the one shaped like a moose?"

"You belong to that moose?"

"Not original I know, seeing as how we border Moose
Lake. It's my uncle's cabin. And his choice of mailbox."

"Why are you living in your uncle's cabin?"

"He offered it to us after my divorce."

He felt her sorrow like the weight of his own. He

flicked his attention from the road just enough to see the last snowflakes gleam as they melted on the soft riotous curls falling around her sweetheart face.

There was sure something about her. It was like a bolt of lightning that hooked straight into his chest. He felt his notorious heart of ice crack a little, and he jerked back, senses reeling as he focused on the road again.

Chapter Two

"You need help getting in?"

Amanda finished the bow on Jessie's hood and made sure it wasn't too tight beneath her chin. "No, but I should at least wipe our snow off your leather seats. I'm guessing that having us drip all over your new upholstery isn't the best thing for it."

"Forget the seats. What about you?" Colt cut the engine and turned to face her. "Looks like your only car is back there in the snowbank. Am I going to leave you stranded here?"

"I have an aunt and uncle in town I can call. Besides, Trusty Rusty's bum radiator is not your problem."

"Radiator? I'm impressed. Not too many women you come across know what's under a car's hood."

"You're looking at a mechanic's daughter. Not only can I change my own oil, but there isn't a mechanic in the western states that can pull one over on me."

"Then why the broken-down car?"

"Oh, I knew you were going to get to that. Not my fault."

"When it comes to women, it never is. At least, in my experience."

"Hey, that sounds a little bitter. You don't come across as a bitter guy."

"Just goes to show appearances can be deceiving."

He'd been hurt. Well, hadn't everybody? Life was like that. She considered their rescuer. For a man over six foot, he wasn't rough looking or intimidating. His jet-black hair was a bit long and tousled, almost out of place with his designer garments and top-of-the-line hiking boots. He looked as out of place parked in front of her modest log cabin as she'd look in the luxury million-dollar homes at the north shore of the lake.

He pocketed his keys, the sure sign of a city boy. Every one here just left the keys in the ignition. "I'll make sure you and your kids get in okay. That there haven't been any more disasters before I leave you stuck here without a vehicle."

"I have—"

"An uncle, I know. What if the phone's out?"

"I have my cell."

"What if there's another dead spot?"

Funny. On one of the worst days of her life, she had to get a ride with a comedian. She gave her Jessie another gentle squeeze. Life was a bittersweet proposition, she was learning. You lived even knowing that one day you would be dying. You loved those you would lose, sooner or later. And the loving and living both had to be done in full brazen knowledge of the loss to come. The trouble was, you never knew how much time you had.

It was even worse when you did.

Don't think about the doctor's prognosis. Amanda was done dealing with bad news—for the day, at least. She forced her mind into a blank so she wouldn't have to face the devastating diagnosis. If she kept moving and didn't do much thinking, maybe she could stay one step ahead of the truth. Denial. It was becoming her favorite state of existence.

Jessie fidgeted against the layers of wool and down. "Don't like the hood, Mama."

"I know, baby. Just a moment longer." She rewrapped the blanket snug and tight, holding her child with care, aware of Colt's gaze on her as tangible as the melted snow cool against her skin. She intentionally avoided his gaze. "Jeremy, zip your coat. *All* the way up."

The kid lurched forward, bumping the backs of the forward seats, as he zipped. "Colt? You know what?"

"What, kid."

"Wonder Boy lives in Los Angeles, too. Do you know him?"

Colt took in the excitement glittering in the boy's eyes. He couldn't remember, had he ever been that believing? "Not anymore."

"Mom, did you hear that?" The boy leaned forward to whisper in his mom's ear, although his words carried above the muted roar of the storm. "He knows superheroes."

"I heard."

That wasn't what he'd meant. Colt opened his mouth

to say so when he caught her gaze. It was as if he could see into her heart through those eyes of hers. See into a sadness that left his soul bleak.

He felt her sorrow like the wind beating against the sides of the truck. This wasn't in his comfort zone, but he let the emotion settle. And he wondered. She'd pulled the scarf over her face again, so only her eyes were exposed. It was as if he could see all of her, right down to her spirit.

This was way too intimate. Much too close. But he didn't blink. Didn't move away. What was it about her that made him see so much? Most people went around with masks firmly in place, right?

"Ready, Jeremy?" She popped open the door, and the blizzard roared into the warm cab.

When he looked next, she was gone.

He followed her into the gale-force winds driving icy pellets against him. Disoriented, he stumbled along the truck toward the faint, twilight shadow of the house.

Where had she gone? He swiped snow from his eyes. There she was, the small child still in her arms, tromping up a narrow walkway toward a wan porch light. The vicious curtain of the storm eased inexplicably around her, as if an angel had reached down to block the worst of the cold from the mother and her children.

He blinked again, sure he was seeing things, but the swirling gray did seem lighter and thinner and the driven snow less cruel when he reached her side. But shrouded in white snow and shadow, Amanda whisked away from him, following her son into the shelter of their home.

This was not a luxury house. Colt took in the details in a flash—the honeyed log walls, the woodstove in the living room, the small rooms, the secondhand furniture. The modest TV in the corner. His heart tugged as Amanda delicately transferred her daughter onto the middle cushion of the decades-old couch, unwrapping her with care. First the coat's hood, then untying the fuzzy hat beneath and tugging off mittens from those small dainty hands.

Colt turned to go, and out of the corner of his eye he saw the muffler come spiraling off…and the mask covering the little girl's mouth and nose. The kind to filter out germs. The kind that very sick people wore.

In the glow of the overhead light, her round button face was ashen and shadowed. Amanda knelt to lift the wool cap from those soft curls, exposing hand-size bald spots between those thin, fine curls.

Air rushed from his lungs. Okay, that was not what he expected. He'd never been around serious illness, but even he could guess at the cause of little Jessie's hair loss. Cancer treatment.

"Would you like some hot chocolate?" Only unmeasured love resonated in Amanda's words as she brushed a hand, tenderly, over her little one's head.

In that moment, gazing down at her daughter, her heart was exposed. He was too far away to hear her words, but he could read her lips. "I love you, baby." And she pressed a kiss to her daughter's cheek.

Unnamed emotion rose in his throat. Colton tore his gaze away to study the cruel tangle of swirling snow outside. The storm beat at the paned glass and scoured the thick log walls, and the wolf's howl of the wind echoed in the icy chambers of his heart.

Okay, new perspective here. He'd been unhappy with his fast-paced, highly successful life. He'd retreated to this corner of God's Country for some R & R.

While he'd had his head down working hard, making money and calling meetings, worrying about stockholders, and profit-and-loss margins and investing more money than any one person ought to have, he'd forgotten a few things that he'd learned long ago.

He watched Amanda step away from the ill child as if her soul was being ripped out of her. The wave of anguish he felt, he realized, was hers, as tangible as the cold rolling from the outside walls of the room. He read the truth on Amanda's face as she kept her gaze from the little girl.

He hung his head. By the grace of God.

It was simple to take for granted the blessings in life. Life was busy and demanding, problem after problem, a hundred things needing to be done in an afternoon.

But it could make a man blind to how he'd been blessed. Through no fault or goodness of his own doing, mostly, but by divine grace. Amanda deserved to have a critically ill child no more than he deserved to be worth hundreds of millions of dollars.

"Where did Jeremy disappear to?" With the microwave beeping in the background, she braced her hands on the scarred Formica counter and looked around. "He opened the door for me. And then what? That kid can disappear in a blink of an eye."

"You need to be careful not to blink, huh?" That had her smiling. "If it helps, there are snowy boot marks tracking through the house."

"Oh, the back door. What on earth did he go back outside for?" If it wasn't one thing, it was another.

Okay, Amanda, start counting. Come back down off the ledge. That's what her mom always said, when she was majorly stressed. Nothing is so bad that it can't get worse.

That wasn't helping. She pressed her fingers to her throat but couldn't feel the gold cross through the layers of turtleneck and wool, but knowing it was there made all the difference. Jeremy hadn't gone far. The car could be fixed. Jessie was still here. Colt had happened upon them at the perfect moment.

She had to take that on faith. No matter how tough things were, someone was watching over them all. That's what she would cling to, anyway, despite any and all evidence to the contrary.

"Would you mind keeping an eye on Jessie while I track down my son?"

The big man standing awkwardly in the middle of the living room looked more like a bear. He was still wearing his parka, unzipped, and the bulky coat added to his already powerful stature. He appeared startled by her request, but he didn't run. "Go ahead. We'll be just fine."

Some men would bolt for the door. Heaven knew that her husband had. But Colt knelt next to the battered end table, switched on a lamp and began sorting through the tall stack of picture books. He chose *The Velveteen Rabbit*. "You like bunnies?"

Jessie nodded once, her big eyes wary.

Okay, now I have to like him. Amanda headed straight for the kitchen and back door to the wintry blast. As snow battered her, she developed a theory where her firstborn had gone off to.

Sure enough, she could see a superhero wrestling with split pieces of firewood he'd taken from the stack in the carport. "Jeremy, leave the wood. You're such a helpful boy, but that's my job."

"I'm Wonder Boy."

"You *are* a wonder, sweetie, but leave the wood and come inside. I was going to make hot chocolate with lots of marshmallows just for you."

"But we gotta keep the house real warm for Jessie."

"I know. That's why we have the modern invention of electric heat. C'mon, kiddo."

"I'm still carryin' this, though. I'm not puttin' it back." He puffed his chest out, determined to do good.

"Okay. Forward march." She laid a hand on his shoulder and didn't let go until she had him safely in the kitchen.

She hadn't been outside more than two minutes, but she was already shivering. The storm was worsening with each passing minute, so much so that the warmth breezing up from the baseboard heaters felt like paradise.

Don't even think about what would have happened if Colt hadn't come along, she thought as she hurried to zap cups of water in the microwave. Jeremy, of course, was already stomping through the house, carrying the two pieces of wood to the box in the living room, leaving enough snow to build two snowmen in his wake.

A masculine baritone rumbled, warm and wonderful. Colt. "That's quite a load you got there."

"Yep. I got this really big sliver. See? It's bleeding and everything."

"Cool."

Male bonding, Amanda supposed. Ice crinkled to the floor as she unzipped her coat and hung it over the back of a chair to thaw. The ear-ringing clatter of wood tumbling into the metal wood bin crashed through the house. Jeremy's announcement, "There. Now I'm gonna make the fire," had her bolting into action, making sure the matches were high out of reach, where they belonged.

They were. Phew.

"That's a man's job, all right. I'm guessing your mom would rather do that," Colt said, calmly, rising from his kneeling position on the floor. All six foot plus of him. "Amanda. We have a problem."

She wasn't exactly sure why her mind had disengaged when that handsome man said her name, but it was as dead as poor Trusty Rusty. "P-problem?"

"Something about a bunny."

"A bunny." It wasn't ringing any bells. Her mind was a total blank. Maybe a total loss. That's it, she'd run over her limit in the ability-to-handle-things department. Plus, it *certainly* didn't help that for the first time she was getting a really good look at Colt, this new neighbor of theirs, in full light.

In the glow of the truck's dash lights, he'd been shadowed, with the twilight of the storm closing in on them. But there was no getting around the fact that he didn't *only* give the impression of being handsome. He was drop-dead gorgeous. From his tousled midnight-black locks to his high, chiseled cheekbones and all the rest of him.

Not that she was noticing. That couldn't be why her brain was stuck in neutral.

It took the desolation of tears filling her daughter's eyes for her mind to kick back into gear. "Oh, her bunny. She always has it with her. Where—" She looked around, lifted a blanket and cast off coats and scarves and mittens.

No bunny.

A vision of the limp-eared pink bunny flashed into her mind. Last seen on Trusty Rusty's backseat. And just how had she forgotten Jessie's toy? Absolute proof that she was losing it. That she was beyond hope of holding it together.

"Let me guess. The car." Colt took an anxious step toward the door.

Not that she blamed him. She was surprised he'd stayed this long. For a bachelor who lived a much faster, more glamorous urban life far from here, he'd done pretty good. Jessie's father had left so fast that he'd been a blur through the back door.

Oops, she'd moved from hopeless to bitter. How had that happened? She definitely needed chocolate. The sooner, the better. "Thanks for the ride, Colt. I—"

"I'll be back." Chocolate-rich, that voice of his.

That just proved she was out on that metaphorical ledge again. Deep down, she so wished for someone strong to lean on—no, that was the wrong word—to lean *against*. A strong, good man who would shelter her while she closed her eyes and leaned against his chest and gathered enough strength from his love to go on.

Fairy-tale wishes, she figured, because the man she'd needed had vanished like smoke.

Now, it wasn't Todd she wanted. It wasn't any man, not even Colt. She closed the door with a final sound that was like a vault's lock clicking shut on her heart.

She was utterly alone. And all out of dreams, too.

Call him temporarily insane. Call it a multiple personality. Call him ashamed. That had to be the reason he had ventured back out into the blizzard. The radio had announced the weather and road advisory—only emergency driving allowed. He'd never seen a blizzard before, much less driven in one.

The truth was, that little girl had gotten to him. And, even more, Amanda. Her sorrow clung to him like the shadows beneath the cedars lining the country road. Not even the gusts battering the side of the truck seemed strong enough to dislodge that sorrow.

Her sweet vanilla fragrance of hand lotion and shampoo faintly circulated with the heater's current in the cab. Maybe that's why she was hard to forget, he reasoned, avoiding thinking of any other possibilities.

He pulled up to the cozy log home mantled in snow and nestled beneath the snow-draped limbs of cedars and fir. Why did his gaze search for her in the window? It was impossible to see anything, except for the blurry haze of light through the torrential snow. Not until he was much closer, standing in the relative shelter of the narrow front porch, could he see her, cuddled on the couch with a child tucked on either side, reading aloud out of a book held open on her lap.

Lamplight haloed them, ringing them with pure golden light, but it was the lovely woman who captivated him. Who made his soul still. He liked how she looked, so genuine and bright.

When she glanced up from her book and their gazes locked, unexplained tenderness came out of nowhere and lit him up from the inside out.

If he were smart, he'd listen to his gut instincts. Get in, leave the stuff and keep going. No involvement necessary. He'd learned the hard way that getting too close to most people only brought you trouble. And nine times out of ten that led straight to grief.

He apparently wasn't that smart, because he couldn't seem to make his feet move or stop the thrum of anticipation as Amanda set aside the book, slipped off the couch and strolled his way.

There was no pretense in her simple appearance, hair falling loosely around her shoulders. She was a slim beauty in wash-worn Levi's, a dark green cable-knit sweater over a turtleneck. And fuzzy yellow slippers on her feet. The whimsical green and red reindeer on the white background of the turtleneck matched her tiny post earrings. A silver charm bracelet full and tinkling swung from her wrist as she strode toward him. It was curious how he noted so many details, since he was never going to see her again, right?

The door swung open. "What are you doing out here, looking like Bigfoot stalking us?"

"Did I startle you?"

"Only a little bit. I'm not really used to strange, muscle-bound men staring in the window at me."

"Hey, I'm not *that* strange."

No, Amanda thought, there was nothing odd about this one. He had honest eyes and an easy, comfortable smile. She had to like him. Who wouldn't? "Is that Brittany Bunny?"

"Affirmative. The rescue mission was successful."

Cold air whirled around her but she hardly noticed it. No, she was too fascinated by this man who towered over her, seeming like everything good in the world. Who'd gone after Jessie's beloved bunny in a worsening storm.

Kindness. The strength of his kindness touched her deeply.

"And when I got in my truck, guess what I found?"

Was she still staring at him? Yes, apparently she was temporarily incapable of speech, too. Embarrassment scorched her face, despite the below zero windchill. *Now* what did she say to the man? He had to think she was a few bulbs short of a full pack. He was holding out her handbag by one strap as if he were afraid her mental condition was contagious.

Not that she blamed him. It had been a long difficult day. And it wasn't over yet. "I apparently left behind something more important than my purse. Somewhere between here and my car, I lost my mind. Let me take that from you and you'll be free of us. Thank God, you're thinking, huh?"

"Not even close."

She took the leather bag by its dangling strap and Brittany Bunny by one lopping ear, and their fingers brushed. She startled at the contact. The strength of it rocked through the insulated layer of his glove. Peace moved into her heart. Even into the hopeless places.

Yep, she was definitely a few bulbs short. And with the door partly open, she was seriously contributing to global warming. The rush of heat slipping by her ankles was in equal proportion to the cold air blowing in. The baseboard heaters clicked on. "You want to come in and warm up?"

"Your back door's unlocked, like everything else around here, right?"

"Yes, but—"

Colt tore himself away, choosing the relative safety of the blizzard. Jumbled up inside, he felt as if the painful tundra that was his heart had taken another mortal crack. Every gut instinct told him to get in his truck and keep going. He was done. Mission accomplished. Time to get back on the road.

But did he listen? No.

Wind-driven snow scoured against his back as he looked over his shoulder. Amanda was gone from the window, gone from his sight. He couldn't say why, but the brightness of her touch remained, calming and terrifying all at once.

He didn't know what he wanted, only that he couldn't walk away.

Yet.

Chapter Three

Okay, so why hadn't he left? Amanda squinted through the glass window in the back door. The six-foot-plus shadow standing on the back porch could only be one man bearing a serious armload of wood, twice what she could usually carry.

She opened the door and was hit by a lightbulb moment. With his forty-thousand-dollar truck and his million-dollar house on the north shore, upscale Mr. Colt had a motive. Charity. Pity. Maybe he was a nice guy, but he was crossing the line.

Either that, or the bitterness was taking on a life of its own.

That's not good, Amanda. Maybe when hope and faith left you, that's what came to fill the void.

"You can close the door now," Colt commented from halfway into the living room.

Great. No wonder he was feeling charitable toward her. She was acting like a space cadet. Pull it together,

Amanda, she thought as she closed the door and slipped through the kitchen to turn on the oven. The trouble was that she wasn't used to having a great-looking, rich, nice, all-around good guy just lend a hand for no good reason.

The phone rang, the cheerful trill rising above the thump as Colt dumped his armload into the bin. The phone rang a second time. A third.

She melted onto the nearby bench, shoved aside the stuff piled there and studied the cordless receiver. She wasn't ready to handle who might be on the other end— not that that was rational. It could be the doctor. Or the doctor's nurse. Or the insurance company with the bad news that they wouldn't cover some of the medical expenses. Her head sank forward into her hands.

Boots tromped to a halt in front of her. She could see those polished, brand-new boots between her fingers.

"Want me to get that for you?"

Her hands began to shake. Or maybe it was her shoulders. She didn't know which. Only that she felt sick with fear down to her soul. *Please, Lord, don't let that be bad news. I'm over my limit for one day.*

Colt grabbed the cordless and squinted at the screen. "It's Edwin Larkin."

"My uncle. I've had a really hard day, that's all," she explained, taking the phone from him. He disappeared back into the storm without comment.

At least she didn't have to worry about him falling desperately in love with her, she thought. One huge worry off her shoulders—not.

"I got your message." It was Ed's wife, Vi, her caring

concern a welcome relief. "Shouldn't she be in the hospital right now? What are the doctors thinking?"

"She was borderline, you know that, and we're hoping she still is. They're waiting on a few test results to see if she needs to be hospitalized." Amanda glanced at the kids, entranced by a children's TV show on the PBS station, and lowered her voice. "I know it's a long shot, but has Uncle Ed heard anything from his friend?"

"Only that Todd's trail in New Mexico has gone cold. He would have called if he'd found something new."

In other words, still a dead end. Amanda leaned her forehead against the cool glass, and tried to summon the wintry temperature into her heart. If she were frozen enough inside, maybe she wouldn't feel the despair filling her up.

"You can't be without a car, dear. Ed's still at the store, but we've agreed to leave you my station wagon."

"No, you do too much already."

"For you and those precious kids, nothing's too much. You know that. And don't think I won't give Dustin at the garage a call. He just serviced that car. He knows little Jessie can't be stranded, as ill as she is."

"He flushed the radiator. Sometimes, even under the best of circumstances, a leak can develop. I keep a close eye on Trusty Rusty's fluid levels."

"I hate to think of you three walking home in this storm. Do you need me to come over? You'll want to warm her up good, with her immune system so compromised."

"She's fine. Trust me." She felt the vibration of approaching footsteps through the glass, opened her eyes and saw the hulking shape of Colt in front of the door. She turned the knob.

"I'm ready to leave. Do you need me to bring anything? Do you have enough groceries to last through the storm?"

"I've got it covered, Aunt Vi."

"See you in two shakes."

Amanda hung up to find Colt on his knees, feeding wood into the fire. Jeremy was at his side, talking animatedly. Probably about Wonder Boy. Colt had made that comment about knowing him, and Jeremy wasn't likely to forget it.

That had to be a good sign the call wasn't bad news, right? Amanda took a shaky breath. It was nearly four-thirty. The doctor had probably gone for the day since it was one of the last few Fridays before Christmas. With any luck, she wouldn't have to face the lab results for her little girl until Monday.

A whole weekend of reprieve. Maybe avoidance wasn't the greatest way to cope, but the doc had been pessimistic. He'd predicted bad news. It was hard to hold on to hope. And she feared it would be bad news— just how bad was the question. The weekend. She would make the most of those days for her kids' sake.

The oven beeped to announce it was preheated. Perfect. Cooking was always a good way to forget her troubles for a bit. She flipped on the faucet and scrubbed her hands.

"Anything else I can do?" The running water had drowned out the sound of Colt's steps.

"Oh, I don't know. Leap a building in a single bound?" She ripped a paper towel from the roll and watched him smile.

Nice smile. Wait, she'd already noticed that.

He leaned against the counter, a life-size superhero in civilian clothes shrinking the limited space in her small kitchen. One brow arched as he studied her. "Are you going to be okay?"

"Sure. As long as that phone doesn't ring with horrible news, I'm good."

"I could unplug it."

"That would only keep it from ringing."

"There's nothing I can do about the news being good or horrible, either way. Would if I could."

Okay, her opinion of him just went up even more. She dug a half-dozen potatoes from the sack beneath the sink. "I've got supper simmering in the Crock-Pot. There's plenty if you'd like to stay—"

"No."

"That was a pretty quick no. I only meant as a thank-you. As a neighborly thing. For all you did today. C'mon. You've got to eat."

"Ah—I've got things to do at home."

"I understand." She scrubbed the potatoes, head bowed, golden tangles of her hair falling forward to hide her face and shimmer in the overhead light.

Colt doubted she had any clue about what was troubling him and why he had to go. Any more cracks to his heart, and it was going to start splintering away. "I'm going to ask again. Are you okay? How about the real truth?"

"That's personal and not pretty."

"Try me."

She glanced over her shoulder to check on her daughter, pulled out a cutting board and loaded the glistening potatoes on it. "You might not have guessed it, but I'm not at my best today."

"I had a hunch." Unexpected tenderness lit him up from the inside out.

"I think I've blown my secret identity. I try to be a very calm mother who can handle everything. But the truth is that I'm not managing that well. I'm a borderline disaster. Your turn."

One brow quirked. "My turn? Oh no, I don't have any secrets. I'm an open book."

"You, sir, are a mystery. I know nothing about you."

"You know everything that matters." He rocked back on his heels. "I'd better go. If it snows any more I'll have to whistle for my reindeer."

Jeremy popped over the other side of the counter, jumping up like a jack-in-the-box. "Know what, Colt? You could stay. Then you could whistle for the reindeer. And they'd fly through the sky and land on our roof."

Colt sighed. He'd only been kidding, but see what he'd inadvertently started?

Amanda shook her head. "Jeremy, stop, please. There will be no reindeer on our roof."

"Aw, Mom."

"Colt, I'd be happy to pack you a dinner to go. That way you get a home-cooked meal and you won't have Jeremy trying to uncover your secret identity."

"I'll pass on the meal, as good as it smells." He spotted a notepad by the phone on the counter. He snatched up the pen resting beside it and scribbled down his cell number. "I'm five driveways down the road, less than half a mile. Call if you need something for your little girl."

"Colt, you don't have to run off."

"Not running. Just want to let you get to your dinner fixing." Panic pounded like laser fire behind his sternum. The scent of a roast and vegetables cooking in a Crock-Pot, the toys in the corner of the living room floor and the woodstove radiating heat, the boy staring up at him with unblinking eyes and the little girl's pale face all knotted him up inside.

A home and a family. Not his comfort zone.

The last thing he saw as he stepped out the door was Amanda, with the dark circles harsh beneath her beautiful eyes and looking like hope lost, waving goodbye.

The emotion that flared to life within him wasn't like anything he'd known before. Like spring's warmth, and as soothing as prayer.

Vicious needles of ice drilled him as he struggled down the walkway bordered by dormant shrubs hunched and draped with snow. The wide lemony squares of windows faded with each step he took. By the time he'd climbed into his truck, the lights had vanished. He was alone in the dark.

He couldn't say if it was longing or relief that haunted him. He'd gotten so used to pushing people away, firmly keeping them at a distance, he wasn't sure if he knew how to trust at all anymore.

When the defrosters had melted holes through the fog and ice on the windshield, he took off, driving as fast as he could, putting distance between him and the little log house and the emotions Amanda and her kids had stirred up. But it was slow going, trying to see through the porthole-sized spot in the windshield like a sailor lost at sea.

By the time he'd reached the snow-covered moose mailbox at the end of the long driveway, he felt safe. He turned onto the main road, inching along, lost in the dark and snow.

"I can see plain as day why you didn't give me a call on that cell phone of yours." There was mischief in Vi's grandmotherly smile as she wiped the newly cleared supper table. The dishwasher rumbled and swished as she swiped down the counters, too. "You can't trust rumors, you know, but I heard the young man who bought the O'Ryan place was single. Handsome. He asked Mabel's granddaughter, the real estate agent handling the sale, about the churches in the area."

Amanda didn't comment as she fetched Brittany Bunny from the couch. "I didn't call you because I'd broken down in the dead zone at the bottom of Rose Hill. I was going to call you when I got reception, but by the time we walked the ten feet, the new neighbor drove up."

"Providential, don't you think?"

"Not that I'd admit it to you." Amanda couldn't help teasing as she crossed to the smallest of the three small bedrooms, thankful for the short hallway that cut off her vision of Vi. That meant the subject of their new neighbor was closed, right? Even if he was a really nice man.

Of course, a lot of men were nice and funny and wonderful and seemingly strong and good-hearted— until you really needed them.

"Here's your bunny." She handed Jessie her beloved toy and smoothed the plump goose-down comforter.

The little girl wrapped her arms around her rabbit,

gave it a hug and sighed. Watery tears stayed in her eyes. Tears of misery.

"My poor baby, not feeling well." She brushed those thin, straggling curls. "Would a story help?"

"The donkey one." She blinked hard against the tears.

Such a good girl. Amanda treasured the sweetness as she chose the picture book with the donkey and the manger and snuggled under the covers with her little girl. She cherished this routine of theirs, cuddling side by side over a storybook, even if Jessie felt too weak to study the colorful pictures carefully. She lay quietly. Gone were the days of bouncing forward to study the illustrations, chatting happily about them. Amanda's heart wrenched so tight, she didn't know how it continued beating.

Please, Lord, stop time from turning. Don't let this end. Amanda knew it was an impossible prayer, but it was what rose up from her soul. She wanted to stay right here, in this precious minute. Where she still had her baby girl.

Just savor this moment, she told herself as she kept reading. Memorize the beloved feeling of holding her child in her arms, the silk of her hair and the sweetness of the way she gave soft, watery sighs at the good parts of the story.

Even as she fought it, the story came to an end. Jessie's heavy eyelids fell and she relaxed into the pillows, lost in sleep. Seconds ticked by, turning into minutes she could not hold on to and freeze-frame so that time stood still.

And in standing still…keep her little girl just like this forever.

An impossible prayer, after all.

Amanda moved with care, tucked the covers snugly around her child, returned the book to its shelf and stood at the foot of the bed, watching Jessie sleep. Holding back all the grief she knew had to come.

For now, she had this moment of grace.

Watch over her, angels, please keep her safe through the night.

I'll be watching, too, she thought, her hand to her throat, where she knew her mother's cross rested beneath the layers of cotton and wool. She longed for her mother sorely. Mom would know just what to do, what to say.

Wanting the weight in her hand, needing the reassurance like air to breathe, she hooked her finger beneath the tight collar of the turtleneck.

No chain. No cross.

No, that can't be right. She yanked hard to stretch the shirt and felt frantically for the familiar links of gold.

Nothing. She caught her reflection faint in the small vanity mirror across the room. Her neck was bare where the necklace used to be. No, not her mother's cross. It was gone. The chain must have broken when she was walking in the storm.

All she had that was left of her mother's, and of her faith, was lost in the dark and the night. Gone.

It's not a sign, she thought as she buried her face in her hands. It can't be a sign. But it was the last straw.

She was all out of everything. Hope, faith, dreams, belief.

Everything.

* * *

Loneliness echoed around him like the darkness, both somehow louder than the howling storm snarling at the walls of his house like a wild beast trying to get in.

Colton wrapped the leftovers of his frozen gourmet pizza and tossed it into the fridge. Vestiges of the day clung to him like the frost on the windows, distorting clear sight.

Today heaven had given him a perception shift that he'd been praying for. Perhaps the saying was true. Be careful what you wish for, you just might get it.

He paced through the middle level of the house, shades drawn against the storm and night. A roomy, luxurious lake home, it was an excellent place to get away from the pressure and stress and unhappy mess his life had become. But there was no relaxing tonight. Maybe it was the weather; he *could* blame his tension on that.

But he'd learned to be honest with himself long ago. It was his conscience and his choices that ate at him in sharp, tenacious bites. He'd come from humble beginnings. He'd worked hard for his success, not for the desire of wealth or power, as much as out of a staunch work ethic and a love of what he did.

His mom had been the one who'd suggested the idea, at the picnic table over charred hamburgers. While handing him the mustard, she'd said, "There should be something better than all those violent video games. Something wholesome. And until there is, Joel, I'm banning your game box station thing from my house."

Of course, Colt's younger brother had complained, but it had gotten Colt to thinking. And now here he was, fourteen years later, with an eight-figure annual salary, his company's stocks one of the hottest in the industry and his biggest problem: pervasive unhappiness. And that was taking him emotionally and spiritually in a direction he didn't want to go.

Amanda. Meeting her—and her kids—left its impression. She'd changed his life today and she didn't even know it. Amazing, the impact one person could have on another's journey.

He leaned over the counter to grab the length of gold chain and a cross he'd found on the floor mat in his truck. Amanda's. The jewelry looked as if it belonged to her—dainty but tasteful. The canned lighting overhead illuminated the piece. Something was etched into the back of the cross, the letters so small he had to squint to read them.

Believe with all your heart.

Oh, he believed. But his faith wasn't polished and gleaming like this cross. It was dusty and tarnished, beliefs he lived and practiced in theory, enough to get by. But he'd stopped living—and believing—with his heart.

You didn't need a heart much, not when it came to building a company. Not to succeed in a competitive, rapidly changing software and computer industry. No, that took a cutthroat mentality and endless hard work. He wasn't much at the cutthroat part, but he was driven. So driven that work was all he had in his life. And his heart, it was as frozen over as the ground outside from lack of real use.

This wasn't the life he'd imagined. The success was nice, he'd been very blessed with that. But he'd always thought he'd end up like most of America—married with kids, a mortgage and a minivan. But he'd been so focused on getting his company off the ground, he'd passed over the chance to be in a serious relationship. Always time for that later, he'd thought.

Now he had the time and no one he could trust. He supposed he was still hurting from his broken engagement. Two years had passed, and he'd never faced the emotional fallout from that. Feelings weren't his thing. So he'd handled it the way he did everything—with work, work, work. That led to more success, and more money, and money could bring out the worst in people. He'd learned that the hard way.

You're not getting what you want, man. He cupped the chain and cross in his hand and made his way into his home office. Not much here, the place was pretty sparse, but in his briefcase he had a few basic tools for emergency laptop repairs. He found a small pair of pliers and bent over the chain. One of the links had stretched open. He fixed it with a quick twist.

Done. Thinking of Amanda did funny things to his chest. Tugged on emotions he wasn't so good at naming. He'd liked being with her. She was spunky, she had spirit and she was all heart.

Being gorgeous didn't hurt, either.

He didn't know what he wanted where she was concerned, but he couldn't ignore the truth. The brightness he felt in his soul when he was with her remained, even hours later. He had a jam-packed life so full of responsibility, his laptop was still up and running, at nine-thirty on a Friday night. He didn't know what he was looking for, only that his life had to change.

He pulled an envelope from his desk drawer. The necklace landed inside with a *plink*. The cross gleamed at him, catching in the light.

Like a sign.

Maybe it wasn't so much that he needed to alter his life, as he needed to transform it. To do everything better. To be better.

And maybe he ought to stop going through the motions, especially when it came to his faith.

Dear Lord, I've had my eyes opened today. And I'm willing. Show me the way, he prayed.

This time he put his heart into it.

Wind scoured snow against the black kitchen window. Amanda doused her tea bag, the brisk scents of black tea, cinnamon and orange rising with the steam. Although she'd left Jessie's side, she hadn't let her out of sight. As she wrung the tea bag, she had a perfect shot through the house and into Jessie's bedroom, where Vi sat at her bedside. The child had woken fretful and ill a few hours ago. It had taken all of her and Vi's patience and care to tend her and soothe her back into a troubled sleep.

"We'll keep her home as long as we can, Amanda," the doctor had said. "But we can only put off hospitalization for so long. You know that. The best we can hope for is to buy a little time and to keep her comfortable."

A little time. *Please, Lord,* she found the prayer rising up from her soul. *Please give us more than that.*

No answer came on this long heartless night.

Not that she expected an answer. Maybe God had stopped listening to her prayers.

Or, perhaps she was the one who could no longer hear. She didn't know anymore.

Vi poked her head around the corner of the hallway, taking a step out of Jessie's room. Exhaustion and worry had weighed down the woman's gentle eyes and stolen the ready smile from her face. "Why don't you take a nap, honey?"

"I can't wind down." Not exactly the truth, since she was drinking black tea to keep her awake, but it was true that if she tried to close her eyes, the worry would start building and make sleep impossible. "The fire needs more wood. I'll make myself useful."

"You need to keep yourself healthy, that's what you need. You need to be strong for your little girl's sake."

"What about you?"

"I'm an experienced med-surg nurse. I worked night shift for ten years before I retired. And now I'm back on duty. It's your turn to sleep. We'll set the alarm if you want to get up and check on her."

"Are you sure you don't want a cup of tea?"

"You can't distract me, dear. I told you. I'm a hardened veteran." But her eyes were kind, seeing all that Amanda did not dare to reveal. "I'll be in here keeping watch. Why don't you take a moment? It's a good time to pray."

"Already been doing that."

She'd prayed so much, she was out of prayers, too. Just repeating the same ones over and over again. Stop time. Slow time. Heal her. Save her. Find a bone marrow donor. Don't take her from me.

Her vision blurred as she knelt in front of the woodstove. When she opened the door, heat and a puff of pungent smoke radiated over her. She worked quietly, adding wood to the flames, so as not to wake the children. As she closed the door again and adjusted the draft, her gaze settled on the bin, still halfway full of wood.

That almost made her smile. Colt. What a lifesaver he'd been today. A total stranger offering his help and then disappearing back into the storm, back to his life. Right when she'd needed help the most.

Maybe God was listening after all, she realized. She couldn't feel Him. She couldn't hear Him. It was hard to sense anything beyond the crushing sorrow and stress in her life right now.

Alone in the dark, she bowed her head and prayed, hoping beyond hope that this time her words would rise all the way to heaven like angels' wings and not go unheard.

Chapter Four

While it was still snowing the next morning, the blizzard had wound itself down. Colton was glad he'd ventured out. He'd never seen or shoveled so much snow, nor had he realized how picture-perfect a good winter storm could make the world. Every flaw, every shadow, every tree was draped in white. You'd hardly know Amanda's car was broken down alongside the road, buried under a new foot of snow and the fresh castoff from the county plow.

The peaceful serenity of the morning stuck with him, even through his errands in town, so did the thought of Amanda's car. It had sure been good and buried. He doubted she had the muscle or the free time to shovel out the sedan. Not that it was any of his business…right? He wasn't sure why he felt that it was. Maybe because he hadn't been able to get her off his mind.

As he crossed the street from the drugstore, which also served as a branch of the post office and a drop-off location for overnight express companies, he felt awareness trickling over him like snow.

Amanda. There she was, right across the street. Sweeping the dry accumulation of snow from the sidewalk fronting the town's candy store. Her head was bent over her work.

There was something about her, beyond a doubt, something that drew him. With every step he took toward her, peace began like a small pinpoint and grew until it shone like the twinkling clear Christmas lights in the shop's window behind her. Tiny crystalline flakes tumbled over her like spun sugar, haloing her blond wavy hair and glossing her shoulders as she worked, making her look even more sweet.

Yeah, he really liked her. "Hey, neighbor."

"Colt." She looked genuinely glad to see him. "What did you think of your first Montana blizzard?"

"It made me glad I had a fireplace and a generator when my electricity conked out." One look at her smile made all sorts of emotions tangle up in his chest. "Are you getting along all right, you and your kids?"

"We've got a woodstove and a generator, too. We're used to weather like this."

She sounded so capable, but he could see that the circles under her eyes were darker than they'd been yesterday, the worry lines etched into her forehead a little deeper. The tangle of emotions in his chest knotted so tight, he couldn't breathe.

"You look surprised to see me. I work here, for my uncle. He owns the shop."

"The shop?"

"We're very popular this time of year. Come in. We have some great specials. Chocolates make perfect Christmas gifts."

"Sure." He realized he was standing in front of a candy store. The rich scent of warm chocolate emanated from the door when Amanda opened it.

"Come in. Uncle Ed won't be happy with me if I let our neighbor turn into an icicle on the sidewalk."

What was it about this woman, that his heart tugged after hers as if attached by an invisible cord? He followed her into the cozy shop, hardly aware of the overhead bell chiming welcomingly and sugar and cinnamon scents whirling in the air like a candy lover's best dream. All of that was background.

"Colt, let me know if I can answer any questions for you. We have all the specials on the board."

What board? He couldn't see anything but her. She filled his senses. He had a hard time finding the words for the question he wanted to ask. He cleared his throat and probably looked like a fool. "You getting along okay without a car? I noticed it was still on the side of the road when I came into town."

"Yes, and it's still buried under all that snow. Ed was good enough to pick me up for work this morning. And Vi's staying with the kids today. Her car is four-wheel drive, so we're doing great."

"Not going to call a tow truck?"

Can't afford to call a tow truck. Not until Monday—payday. Amanda bit her lip before the words popped out. Not his problem. Life had seen fit to hand her so many problems, she was determined to handle each and every one of them to the best of her ability. "I'll get around to it soon enough. Now, we ship—"

Something gleamed in the flat of his palm. A liquid puddle of gold links and—

"The cross." She blinked. It was still there, held patiently in his wide hand. "No, this is impossible. How could you— I mean, I thought it was lost forever." Stop babbling, Amanda, she told herself. "I just can't believe it."

"I found it in my truck. One of the links had popped open, so I fixed it. Good as new."

Tears burned in her eyes, blurring her vision. "This is too good to be true."

"You seem pretty glad to see it. It must mean a lot."

"This was my mom's. Some days it feels like my only connection to her."

"She's passed?"

A single nod.

"Yeah, my mom, too."

"So you know." She felt her heart open up, usually so guarded, moved by the comparable pain in his dark gaze. She wanted to tell herself it was sympathy for his loss that made her take a step closer. In truth she didn't know if he was the one affecting her, or if it was seeing the cross again.

"Here, let me," he offered, lifting the links of chain by the clasp.

"Thanks, I'm trembling. It's just—" You're babbling again, Amanda. Her breath caught as he towered close and hooked the chain securely at her nape. He smelled great, like winter wind and fresh snowy forests. "Thank you."

"My pleasure." His gaze held hers, and the honest force of it left her even more paralyzed by awe.

Her soul stirred in a new and different way. Confused, she stepped back. Surely he was just being kind, *again,* that was all. She was letting him affect her way too deeply, but oh, it felt good to have the slight, reassuring weight of the cross at her throat. "How am I going to repay you now, after this?"

"Just add it to my tab."

"I must be about maxed out, over my limit."

"Not even close."

"Then how about a box of chocolates, my treat?" She backed away. "Here, have a sample. It will tempt you into accepting my offer."

He studied the dark chocolate cordial she held out to him in a small holly leaf patterned paper. "You play hardball."

"That's me." She slipped the chocolate on its bed of paper onto the top of the display case. Slid it closer to him. "Go on. You haven't tasted better candy. It's Uncle Ed's secret recipe."

It wasn't the chocolate that had him staying. He'd returned the necklace to her, so time for him to leave. But instead of walking out the door, like a sensible man, he accepted the treat.

Why this woman, he wondered. Why her? Maybe because he could see right through to her true spirit. She was unpretentious. She wore no veneer, no masks, just an open caring heart. He'd never been so awed by anyone.

"What do you think, Colt? Fantastic chocolate, right?"

Yep, that was the word he wanted. Fantastic. But it

had nothing to do with the tastes of blissfully sweet blueberry and dark chocolate on his tongue.

Across the counter, beneath the glow of the white twinkle lights, she withdrew a box, prewrapped and topped with a gold foil bow. "Our finest huckleberry cordials. Those are our local berries. They're like blueberries, but they're much sweeter. They grow wild right up to our deck."

The information was hardly registering. His senses were buzzing. His heart cracked right open, leaving him exposed and vulnerable. Not something he'd felt before, either, although he suspected he knew exactly what this feeling was.

Unaware, Amanda slipped the candy box into a bag with paper handles. "Huckleberries are best ripe, fresh off the bush. Last summer we could eat our fill without getting out of our chairs. This summer you can probably do the same from your deck—"

"Colt! Colt!" With a bang of the door, the jar of the bell, the sound of stampeding feet on the wood floor, Jeremy bolted into the shop, an elderly man on his tail. "Know what? I saw the new Wonder Boy comic! It's in the bookstore an' everything."

"Is that right, kid?"

Amanda left the bag on the counter, listening as the boy and man exchanged speculations on Wonder Boy's latest adventures. She didn't miss her uncle's quirked brow or the spring in his step as he shucked off his parka and took his place behind the register.

"Oh, I know what you're thinking," she muttered, keeping her voice low. "Leave the poor man alone."

"He's got no wedding ring." Ed winked. "Is that the fellow Vi told me about? He's some big important businessman. Paid cash for the O'Ryan place. Sure seems to get along with Jeremy."

"He found Mom's cross. That's why he's here. That's it."

"That's not it. I saw the way he was looking at you."

"It wasn't me. He had his first blueberry cordial. Everyone looks like that when they eat your specialty chocolates." Really, as if she was in any way attractive to a well-to-do bachelor. With debt up to her eyeballs, an active boy and a critically ill little girl, she wasn't the ideal catch for any man. If her husband hadn't been able to stay when times got tough, there was no way any other man would even look at her twice.

Not that she blamed them. "I'm doing fine on my own."

"I know you are, pumpkin. That don't mean that nice fellow right there isn't the answer to my prayers for you."

"Oh, Uncle Ed." He could make her heart melt. "Why couldn't I find a man as wonderful as you?"

"Every woman who comes in here asks that. It's because of my secret chocolate recipe." He winked, teasing, when the truth was, she didn't know where she'd be without Ed and Vi.

She didn't want another husband, anyway. What she wanted was for her daughter's test results to come back with miraculous improvement. What she wanted was for Jessie never to have fallen ill in the first place.

When she looked up, Colt was watching her over the top of Jeremy's cap. Great. What if he'd overheard the thing Uncle Ed had said? Heat crept across her cheekbones. What did he see when he looked at her? A single mom doing her best to hold it together—that's what he saw. He probably thought she was looking for Husband Number Two.

But when she looked at him, she didn't see a marital candidate for her. She saw a man who was strong, patient and kind. Who liked kids, obviously, or he wouldn't be talking so earnestly with Jeremy. Why hadn't he married? Why didn't he have a family of his own? Not that it was her business, but a girl could wonder.

Maybe she ought to rescue him from her son. She grabbed the bag of chocolates and delivered them. "Is he wearing your ears out, yet?"

"Nope." Colt's knuckles brushed hers as he took the bag.

Wow. Her touch made his soul still. He couldn't blame the reaction on the chocolate this time. Not even close.

"Jeremy," she said in her gentle alto. "Time to come with me. I've got ribbons to tie for the boxes. I need a superhero's help."

"Aw, Mom."

"Colt's a busy man. I'm sure he has a lot of important things to do." There was no mistaking her love as she ruffled her son's hair.

"What could be more important than Wonder Boy?" Colt asked.

Earning a grin from Jeremy, and an appreciative smile from his mom.

Colt knew he was in trouble as Amanda took a step

away, and he felt the tug of his heart as if she were taking a piece of it with her.

"Mom, I just gotta tell him one more thing!"

"Okay, but then let the man go." Amanda paused at a door in the back. "See you around, Colt."

"Sure thing."

He had to admit the truth. He cared for her. It wasn't a conscious decision. It was simply there.

"I know your secret. Your real identity."

Colton whipped around, startled by the little boy, who had followed him to the door. "My real identity, huh?"

"Sure. I know all about 'em. You're like Wonder Boy. When he isn't doing good, he's Wade Moss, mild-mannered business student. Right?"

So his secret was out. He figured the real estate agent had already spread the rumor: extremely rich guy buys vacation house. It accounted for all the unmarried women in the grocery store who'd tried to get his attention. Not that he was interested.

What interested him was the one woman who wasn't trying to get his attention. His gaze cut to the back of the store, but she'd already disappeared from sight.

That's when he noticed the display by the door. A coffee can with a slit in its plastic lid perched on the edge of a cloth-covered table. A computer-generated sign hung on the wall above it. Please Help Us Raise Money For Our Niece's Medical Expenses.

Jessie. He remembered Amanda's look of love when she held her daughter. It wasn't even a thought, he was already pulling his wallet from his back pocket and emptying the folds of hundred-dollar bills into the can.

"Wow!" Jeremy stared up at him as if he'd just leaped to the moon in a single jump. "I knew it! I go around doin' good, too. I help my mom and my sister all the time."

Now, *that* humbled him. How long had it been since he'd thought about going around doing good? He'd been Jeremy's age. "You keep being good. Okay?"

"Like you?"

"Not me, kid. I could be doing things better. Your mother's looking for you." He could see her through the store, and he felt ashamed, because that money, as much as it was, was pocket change to him. No big sacrifice. Thinking about that, he opened the door. "See ya around, Jeremy."

"Cool! Bye, Colt!"

As he strolled the sidewalk to his truck, parked not far away, he caught a blur of pink—a woman's pink sweater—moving beyond the shop's front window. Amanda, probably come to retrieve her son.

As Colt jogged across the street, fishing his keys from his jacket pocket, a strange connection—a mood—brushed through his soul. Maybe it was her mood, maybe it was his own, he didn't know, but he didn't look up as he unlocked the door. Inside the truck she was safely out of his sight. Snow draped the windows like a thick white sheet.

In the quiet, Jeremy's words came back to him. *You're like Wonder Boy. When he isn't doing good, he's Wade Moss, mild-mannered business student. Right?*

Wrong, kid. He started the engine and hit the defroster on high, remembering what he'd told the boy. *I could be doing things better.* He didn't know if the kid thought rich guys did a lot of charity work or something, but it was almost as if Jeremy thought he was like Wonder Boy. A secret doer of good.

Not even close.

He grabbed his ice scraper and hopped outside to start clearing his windows. There was a faint blur of pink in the shop across the street. His chest wrenched, as if tough layers of hard ice were wrenching apart. The crisp brush of snowflakes against his face seemed to urge him to look again, toward the cozy little candy store.

He swore he heard the wind whisper, this is the way.

Amanda could barely hear the knock over the children's Christmas carols playing on the small CD player. Since she was in the middle of unstringing the tangled mass of Christmas-tree lights, she was a little tied up. If she let go of the carefully uncoiled section, there'd be utter disaster. She'd have to start all over again. "Jeremy, get the door, please."

"The door?" He'd been jumping up and down, tossing handfuls of tinsel into the air, not that it was helping with the tree decorating process, but he'd made Jessie sit up in her chair and laugh. Priceless. What was a mess on the floor compared to that?

Since he was wearing his Wonder Boy T-shirt, he flew over an open box of ornaments and yanked open the door.

"Hey there, Wonder Boy," rumbled a familiar baritone. "Is your mom home?"

"Yeah, but she's real frustrated."

Amanda rolled her eyes. Leave it to Jeremy. She

gave the string of lights a good yank, but it only tangled more. "I'm not frustrated. Just patience-challenged."

He strolled into sight, holding up a big brown bag. The door swept closed behind him. "Good thing I swung by the chicken place."

"You really have to stop being so generous to us."

"I can't. It's getting to be a habit."

"You got a bucket of chicken?" Jeremy leaped again. "Potato wedgies, too?"

"Can't eat fried chicken without 'em," Colt said.

And stole her heart. She was a softie when it came to anyone genuinely nice to her kids. "Small problem. Aunt Vi wants to bring supper over. I'll just give her a call—"

"Who do you think told me what kind of chicken to buy? I got her number from your uncle. I called his store to buy some more of those cordials—and send them for gifts. That's quite a mess you've got."

"Last year's Christmas was kind of hectic. I just unwound the lights from the tree and stuffed them in a bag. Big mistake."

"So I see. Jeremy, fly this into the kitchen for me, would ya?" He held out the bag, making sure the boy had a good hold on it before the kid leaped away, always helpful. The big mountain of a man knelt down before her. "Nice tree."

Amanda's breath caught as he leaned close to take the other end of the string of lights. He bent his head over his work, his big, capable hands efficiently untangling the plug from the rest of the coiled mess. She *had* to stop noticing just how handsome he was.

Wait, hadn't he asked her a question? Heaven help

her, her brain had short-circuited again. Oh, right, he'd said something about the new tree, a freshly cut five-foot spruce tucked in the corner by the window. "Uncle Ed's son dropped this by from his tree farm. He was making deliveries in the area. He found the perfect one for us, didn't he, Jessie?"

The little girl nodded, cuddled up with a blanket and pillow, a makeshift bed in the overstuffed chair.

The little girl's skin looked more translucent today, emphasizing the shadows beneath her eyes. Colt remembered the collection can. He owed this child. She'd given him a new perspective, one he was determined not to forget. Maybe he could repay her—he'd think on that. He glanced at the clock on the wall near the door. The mechanic ought to be coming by any minute.

"Maybe this year I'll get a Christmas tree." He looped the plug through a knot and watched Amanda.

"What do you mean, *this* year? You celebrate Christmas, right? Vi said the real estate agent said that you asked about the local chur— Wait. Scratch that. I can't believe I did that. I'm actually listening to gossip about you and I repeated it in front of you. I'm more tired than I think."

She looked more exhausted, too. With the way her attention kept cutting past him to the ill child propped up in the chair, he wasn't surprised. He doubted if Amanda could let Jessie out of her sight long enough to get any decent amount of sleep.

"So, you've been checking up on me?" he asked.

She blushed. "It's Vi. She felt compelled to volunteer all this stuff she heard about you."

"Stuff, huh?" He studied the little girl again, so unnaturally still and ashen.

All money could do was buy medical treatment for her. But if that wasn't enough, then all the riches in the world would be without value.

"Don't worry. Your bachelor status is safe from me." Amanda studied him through her lashes. "I'm not looking for a second husband."

"Didn't think you were."

"I see how you look at me."

As if he was looking at Christmas? She hadn't guessed, had she? Had he been *that* transparent? "How do you mean?"

"With a little bit of panic."

Whew. He chuckled in relief. "Not for the reasons you think. I've been burned pretty bad. It makes a man wary."

"Is that why you bought a vacation home in Montana?"

"No, there's no Mrs. I've left behind in California. I haven't taken *that* step. I've gotten close to marrying—once—but when I got to the truth of who she was beneath the polish and the pretense, she was purely a gold digger."

"I'm sorry. That had to hurt."

"Not as much as if I'd found out after the wedding. It happened a few years ago. I've recovered. Maybe not from the bitterness. I'm working on that."

"I'm working on the bitterness, too." She stared hard at the tangle in her hand. "I was afraid that you'd overheard what Uncle Ed was saying while you were in the shop."

"Jeremy and I were deep in discussion. Why, what did your uncle say?"

"You don't wanna know, trust me. But if he happens to say anything cryptic, it's not coming from me. He means well. He's like a father to me. The only thing I want in this world is for Jessie to feel better. Right, baby?"

A weary nod.

Yeah, he already knew.

Jeremy bounded back into the living room. "Mom! There's a big truck outside. It's Dustin's tow truck! And he's pullin' our car."

"What? That can't be right. Can it?" She abandoned the lights, rising up, a few silver sparkles of tinsel falling off her as she headed to the window. "I didn't call. Ed promised he'd take a look at the radiator after he closed the store—"

Colton caught Jeremy's broad grin and gave him a wink. He laid a finger to his lips, a reminder to keep their secret.

Jeremy nodded, his eyes shining, and took his mom's hand.

Chapter Five

"It's good to see the Trusty Rusty back in service," Vi commented as she burst through the kitchen door, bringing the scents of winter wind, crisp snow and cake with her. "It must not have been anything serious. Always a good sign. We met Dustin in his tow truck on the driveway. He must have just delivered it."

Amanda hurried to relieve her aunt of the plastic cake carrier. "Yeah, the funny thing was that the bill was already paid. You wouldn't know anything about that?"

"Not me. Ed was going to dig it out and take a look, but by the time he got to it, he said it was gone. Nothing but a spot alongside the road where it had been." Vi shrugged out of her winter coat and hung it on the tree by the door. "I whipped up a little dessert. When that nice young man of yours—"

"He's not mine," Amanda patiently corrected. While it irked her, she knew there would be many more match-making comments to come. And here she was, already patience-challenged from dealing with the tree lights. "Angel food. Jessie's favorite."

"Don't try and change the subject on me, missy." Vi wrapped her in a hug. "I'm a veteran when it comes to getting to the truth. How are you holdin' up, honey?"

"You know me. Holding on with what's left of my fingernails, but I'm holding on." Amanda glanced over the counter to where Jessie was giggling at Jeremy, who'd dropped a clump of tinsel on top of his head and danced around like a mock ballerina.

Sweet love for her children brimmed, and she felt a tad bit stronger. Colt was safely out of earshot, keeping one eye on Jeremy and the other on the lights he was working on. "About the car, Vi. It was wonderful of you to fix the car, but I'm paying you back."

"That wouldn't be possible, seeing as how we didn't do anything to the car."

"But Dustin said the new radiator was paid for. When I asked by who, he said it was a secret. That sounds like something you and Ed would do. Especially since the mechanic fixed Trusty Rusty the same day? That never happens anywhere in the known universe."

"Know what I think? Word must have gotten around to Dustin, that's my guess. He's a good fair man, but this is a small town and he knows that folks will hear how your car broke down right after he worked on it, saying it was in tiptop shape. And with Jessie so sick 'n all, why, he's gonna do the right thing. That's all this is." Vi unrolled the take-out bag on the table. "My, isn't this somethin'? What a treat, not to have to cook."

"He can hear you, Vi."

"Yes, I can," Colt confirmed from the living room floor. "Amanda, do you want me to start stringing the lights? Or do you want the honor?"

"Let me guess. You're not a veteran at this. I remember that crack you made about maybe getting a Christmas tree."

"I figure I can run my own business, I can put lights on a blue spruce."

"Be my guest, but don't say I didn't warn you."

"Fair enough."

He looked like the kind of man a woman could count on. Maybe it was those shoulders of his, wide and so capable, or maybe the granite look of him. It was nice. Very nice.

Not that she was even at a place where she could *think* about being interested in dating and marriage again. But a man like Colt could make her want to wish—in spite of everything.

Not that she was wishing.

Vi paused on her way into the living room. "He looks like a very good man to me."

"He certainly does. We're blessed to have such a nice neighbor. Colt, prepare yourself. This is my aunt Vi."

Amusement danced in Vi's hopeful eyes. "Aren't you helpful? You need any help with those lights?"

"Wonder Boy and I got it covered. Good to meet you, ma'am."

"Handsome and polite, too," Vi whispered before she charged into the room and gave Jessie a raspberry smooch on her cheek.

"Aunt Vi!" Jeremy called from behind the tree. "I'm helpin'."

"And what a good job you're doing, too," Vi praised as she snuggled Jessie on her lap.

There was a bump at the back door. Amanda raced to turn the knob as Ed blew in with the wind and an armload of wood.

"Just thought I'd bring in a load since I was comin' this way," he explained as he stormed toward the woodstove. "It looks like Christmas in here."

Jeremy leaped, the tree's boughs swinging in his wake, and rushed to the older man's side, talking a mile a minute. At the same moment, Colt knelt to plug in the first string of lights and Jessie's eyes danced with pleasure at the sight. For a brief instant, her illness was forgotten, her joy transcended everything.

Amanda tried to take a picture in her mind, to capture what was dear about this exact minute. The scent of wood smoke and fresh spruce, the thump of Jeremy's feet as he leaped and bounded, the warmth of family gathering. Most importantly she wanted to memorize the way Jessie lit up, wonder transforming her cherub's face. Bright, happy blue eyes. Her silken red-gold curls so perfectly framing her face. The beloved way she clasped her little hands together, and the gasp she made when Colt fiddled with the lights and they began to blink. Pink, yellow, purple, blue and green sparkled and danced over the low branches.

Time, it just kept slipping by. Sorrow speared so sharply into her soul, she couldn't bear it. Don't think about it, Amanda. Just think about this moment. Appreciate this moment. This, right here, is what's important.

She pressed her hand to her mother's cross, familiar and precious, and thought of the words inscribed there. She would believe, with all her heart, even when her heart was no longer whole.

She wrenched away from the sight, battling down the sorrow, and counted off enough plates from the stack in the upper kitchen cabinets.

"You okay?" Colt's broad hand settled on her shoulder.

She hadn't heard him approach, but there he was at her side, his touch radiating peace and comfort like nothing she'd ever known. What was it about this man? She hardly knew him, and yet it was as if her soul did.

Which just showed how sleep deprived she was. She didn't believe in soul mates. Or in love at first sight. What she wanted to believe was that not all men ran when things got tough. That not all men caved instead of standing tall.

"I'm managing." She slipped away from his touch, pivoting to set the plates on the table. Jeremy had turned the overhead lights off in the living room and the jeweled glow of the twinkling lights felt almost like hope, battling against the dark.

There was a tug of a drawer opening, then thumping shut. Another opening. She heard the clink of flatware. Colt, helping to set the table. In the living room, Jeremy was chatting earnestly with Ed, and Jessie's eyes had begun to droop as she was cradled in Vi's arms.

Colt brushed against her, as solid as granite. "You're worried she won't be home for Christmas."

She couldn't nod. She couldn't move. The wave of sorrow returned with tsunami force.

"Oh." He laid his hand to his heart, as if he knew the words she could not allow to form, not in her thoughts and not in words.

"That's only ten days away."

"Three weeks ago, she was safely in remission." Amanda took a step back, afraid he would reach out to her. Afraid he would offer, even as a neighbor and a friend, to hold her while she cried.

Well, she wasn't about to cry, and she refused to lean on any man. Not so easily again.

"What are her treatment options?"

"The one thing that has a good chance of curing her is a bone marrow transplant, but we don't have a donor."

"I thought siblings usually were matches. Isn't Jeremy?" He paused as she shook her head. "You?"

She turned away in silence. "Not in the national registry, either. We don't know about her father. He could be a match. Maybe not. Who knows? He took off early in her illness. Ed has a friend who's a private eye, but he hasn't found Todd yet. So here we are, taking one day at a time and trying to make it the best day we can."

"Is there anything I can do?"

"You can pray."

Colt watched, helpless, as she managed a determined smile, strolled into the front room and, as if her heart was whole and filled with hope, called everyone to the table.

When he'd been stringing lights on the tree, he tried to remember the last time he'd been as content and relaxed. Couldn't do it.

And now, in the space of minutes, he couldn't rightly breathe for the absolute sorrow gathering inside him.

* * *

"Which color do you want to put on next?" Amanda waited, holding her child tight, never wanting to let go. She had Jessie choose from the nearly empty boxes of ornaments set open on the living room side of the kitchen counter.

"Purple."

"Okay. Purple it is." She snagged a plastic green hook from the container tucked between the boxes, hooked it through the last purple ball and gave a tug. Nothing. The ball was good and wedged in its formfitting plastic holder. Oops, she needed two hands.

"Allow me, ladies." Colt brushed behind her, as solid as an iron tower. But it was his kindness that she noticed—couldn't stop noticing—as he pulled the ball free.

Her spirit stirred when his fingers covered hers. Of course she liked this very masculine, very capable and thoughtful guy. Who wouldn't? But when his hand remained on hers a few long beats, she didn't know what to think. When he pulled away, sweetness welled up through her soul.

"Let's put this on the tree, baby." Trying to act unaffected, she carried her daughter to the bright corner, where the well-appointed Christmas tree blinked and sparkled.

"Where do you want to put it?"

Jessie pointed, and Amanda slipped the hook over the tip of the designated spot.

"Tinsel, Jess!" Jeremy tossed another handful ceilingward, and it sparkled as it fluttered down, snowing over them all.

Jessie held out her little hand and caught a gleaming

strip like a falling star. It glowed purple and yellow and pink, reflecting the closest tree lights. For one moment, there was simply joy.

Amanda pressed a kiss to her daughter's temple. There wasn't enough time to pack all the joy into the time ticking away. Not enough sweet kisses. Not enough hugs. Not enough anything.

A hundred prayers whispered from her soul. Prayers for a change in the progression of Jessie's illness. For another remission. For a donor. Those prayers remained silent, held deep in her heart.

Don't look ahead, Amanda. Don't expect the worst, or the best. Just hold on to this moment.

Jessie tossed the tinsel. It lifted upward like a perfect prayer and landed with a swish on an upper tree branch, colorful and bright.

"Look how pretty," Amanda praised. "Good job, baby."

Aunt Vi hurried out from the kitchen with a tray of gingerbread cookies and warm cinnamon apple tea and cocoa.

Ed held up the last ornament. "What should I do with this one, missy?"

Jessie pondered the situation carefully and pointed.

"Ain't that the perfect spot," Ed complimented, as he slid the sparkling pink ball onto the last available branch.

Jeremy dropped a handful of tinsel on top of it for good measure.

Colt could clearly see the shadows in Amanda's deep, still eyes. He could see her breaking heart as surely as the dense night shadows crept through the room.

He could also sense her gladness. Her words came

to him like a prayer's answer. *So here we are, taking one day at a time and trying to make it the best day we can.*

Something more powerful than tenderness filled him up, making it impossible to breathe or blink or move. It felt as if the floor shifted beneath his feet. His gaze found her on the other side of the tree, framed by the jewel-rich tones of the lights, the soft green boughs and his heart. He felt changed. He didn't know why now or why this woman. Only that it felt like the Lord's leading.

And his soul finding its match.

"Look," she said, speaking to her daughter, but her gaze held his. "Colt has the tree topper. Maybe he'll put it on for us."

Colt looked at it, trying to figure out how to go on normally from here. Everything felt changed—in a single moment—and time continued on, everything looking the same as it had been: the expectant faces of Amanda and her family, the crackle and pop of the fire in the stove, Jeremy's energy as he grabbed hold of the chair back.

Only Colt—his heart and soul—had changed.

He felt wooden as he lifted the delicate glass ornament. It took a moment to slip it into place and clip in the electrical plug. Soft, pure white light shone down like grace. Colton took a step back, looking up at the fragile angel dressed in silver and gold, hovering above the tree like hope.

In the radiant light, Amanda held her child, and he felt her prayers as if they were his own.

Ed left with a friendly goodbye, and Colton figured he ought to do the same. Vi was spending the night, helping Amanda in the bedroom with the little girl. It was time to go, but he didn't want to leave without saying good-night. He snared a gingerbread man from the platter on the table.

"Colt?" Jeremy gazed up at him, errant pieces of tinsel shining in his tousled hair. "Know what?"

"What, buddy?"

"I gotta ask you somethin'."

"It's real important, I can see that." He pulled a chair from the kitchen table. "Shoot."

"Okay, I, uh—" Jeremy fidgeted from one foot to the other, worry lines digging into his forehead. "I gotta know. Uncle Ed says that Santa Claus is specular."

Whatever he'd been expecting the kid to ask, this hadn't been it. He wasn't sure what to say. He hadn't given Santa much thought in, oh, the last twenty-four years. "Do you mean secular?"

"Is that real bad? 'Cuz he gives stuff to kids, like Jessie and she's sick. And that's being good. He's like a superhero, right? 'Cuz he can fly the whole world in a single night."

"Those are some pretty serious questions."

"Yeah." Burdened, Jeremy plopped down on the chair next to him and propped his chin in his hands. "I kinda figured you'd know."

"Why? You got a letter to send him or something?"

Jeremy bit his bottom lip and rolled his eyes to the ceiling, apparently thinking real hard. Apparently not knowing what to ask, or how to say it.

Colton sensed her before he saw her, padding from the shadowed hallway and into the light. She looked lovely in a pink fuzzy sweater and jeans. Her mom's cross hung at her throat and glinted like a sign.

He wasn't sure if she felt what he did. He couldn't tell it by any change in her expression. She stopped short, though, keeping a fair distance between them. There was only friendliness and warmth in her voice. "Colt. You weren't going to leave without saying goodbye to me, were you?"

"No way. I was just gnawing on a cookie and discussing important matters with Jeremy."

"So I see." She looked luminous in the soft light. "I hate to interrupt man talk, but Jeremy, your bath is ready."

"Aw." Jeremy snapped his fingers. "Mom, me and Colt're talkin'."

"You can talk to him another time. Say good-night and scoot."

"Oh, okaaay. 'Night, Colt."

"'Night, buddy."

He took off in leaps and bounds through the room and into the hallway. A door bumped shut.

"Nice kids you got."

"Thanks, I think so, too. They're the best things that ever happened to me."

Yeah, he could see that. "I had a real nice time. Thanks for letting me drop in."

"Anytime. Thanks for bringing supper."

"My pleasure." He rose out of the chair to tower over her, and the atmosphere changed, like the snap of electricity in a lightning storm.

That sweet longing she'd felt earlier returned, rushing into life out of nothing at all, so strong and bright it blotted out her pain and fears. She cared for him; she couldn't help it. She liked Colt. She liked him very much.

As a neighbor. As a friend. There could be nothing else between them. She took a step away, her background thoughts remaining on the child in her bedroom. Vi was with her and was reading her to sleep. There was no other place Amanda wanted to be than to be watching over her daughter. And yet, she felt an unexplained need to talk to Colt a little longer. To be in his presence.

To again feel the peace his touch had brought to her.

Goodbye was on her lips, but Jeremy's muffled voice from the bathroom stopped her; he was singing the theme song of his favorite superhero. "He's in a Wonder Boy phase. I'm not sure how long it's going to last."

"I've still got mine, from when I was a kid."

"I guess we all need heroes in our lives."

"Yes, we do." His gaze went dark, inscrutable, as he reached out to smooth a stray lock of hair from her cheek and tucked it behind her ear.

A tender gesture. One that tugged at the wishes locked deep within her. Amanda squeezed her eyes shut, gathering all her willpower to take one step back. "Good night, then."

He left in silence. There was a muted click of the back door, and she was alone in the kitchen, the scent of his aftershave a reminder of his presence. The sting of lost dreams lingering in the shadows.

"M-mom?"

The thin frightened voice of her son wobbled in the dark.

Amanda startled, straightening up in the chair by her daughter's bed. Thankful for the shadows that hid the way she swiped tears from her eyes.

The luminous green numbers on the bedside clock showed it was after three in the morning. Taking care not to wake Jessie, who'd finally fallen back asleep, she rose and padded into the hallway. A night-light shone at the baseboard, casting just enough of a glow to see by.

"Are you cryin'?"

Best not to answer that. "Wh-hat are you doing up, young man? You should be sound asleep."

Stocking feet padded closer into the faint glow from the night-light, enough to see the worry dug deep into his forehead. "I—I was gonna check on Jessie."

"You don't have to worry, I'm watching over her. Vi's here, too."

"I know." So much heartache in his voice as he wrung his hands. "Is she gonna have to go to the hospital again?"

"It looks like it. We'll keep her here as long as we can."

"I'm Wonder Boy. I'm gonna burn up all the cancer with my laser vision."

"If only it were that easy, baby." She pulled him into her arms, treasuring the sweetness of this good boy she'd been given. "Now, back to bed. Wonder Boy needs his sleep so he can fight doom tomorrow."

"Okay, 'cuz I'm gonna fix it. Mom, you like Colt a lot, right?"

Sure, she saw what Jeremy was thinking. The boy missed his father. He also missed *having* a father. The last thing she wanted was for him to start hoping for the impossible. Colt was…*fine*. No doubt about that.

But…well, there were too many buts. Too many reasons. "He's a good neighbor, isn't he?"

"He knows lots about superheroes."

"You know he'll be going back to California soon, where he lives full-time. He just visits here a few weeks a year."

"I know, Mom, but he's *super.*"

Yeah, no argument there. If things were different, it would be simple to care more for him. In a way that went beyond neighborliness.

But her life wasn't different. "You're still not in bed, mister."

"Yeah, I know, but…" He bit his lip, thinking hard. "I'm gonna ask for help."

"Good plan. Praying is always a good thing when you need a miracle as much as we do."

"I know, Mom."

She leaned through the doorway to check on Jessie, still sound asleep, before following her son into his room. He jumped into bed and threw himself under the covers. How he had so much energy at this time of night was a complete mystery.

"Sleep tight." She bent to kiss his brow, so grateful for him and Jessie. No matter how tough things had been or would get, she wouldn't trade them for anything.

Maybe that was life, always a balance, always the love and the loss, the light and the dark, the sweet and the bitter. But the one thing she knew for sure was that it was a privilege to be here. A privilege to care for her children, for better or worse.

She heard Jeremy muttering a prayer as she closed

his door. And went back to Jessie's room, to check on her, but Vi was there, too, watching over her.

Please, don't take her from me. She felt lost and alone. The wind gusted with despair at the eaves, making the night shadows seem darker as she made her way down the hall. The tree lights were still on, although the rest of the room was dark. The angel shone as bright as a holy star, a steady light in the inexorable darkness.

Amanda reached for the switch for the tree lights and paused, the angel hovering above. Maybe she'd leave it on for a while longer. She needed all the inspiration she could get.

She felt for her mother's cross, familiar and comforting enough to warm her heart. She knew the words etched on the back; so many times had she studied them, she could see the perfect image of those tiny, script letters.

Even when she was drowning in unanswered prayers. Even when she was standing without hope, so alone she could feel the empty place within her where her faith used to be.

She would still believe.

Chapter Six

Sunday morning dawned quietly behind medium gray clouds. Facing a wide picture window, Colton had a perfect view at his desk, over the top of his laptop.

As he sipped his first cup of coffee, the frozen, solemn world began to change. The line of mountains and trees took shape and hue and stood in harsh, green-black relief against the leaden sky.

By his second cup of coffee the snow that shrouded east to west, north and beyond had turned incandescent, radiating as if with its own light, like white foil on mountaintops and treetops and the long line of lawn sloping away from his house. Not a creature moved, or wind or breath or leaf; there was only complete, sacred peace.

As he waited for his modem to connect, he noticed an odd blur in the woods along the edge of his property. Perhaps deer or elk or moose—the real estate agent had promised wildlife sightings.

Except deer didn't usually wear red, did they?

Suspecting whoever was out there was not of the wildlife variety and more likely a grade school kid he'd gotten to know, Colton left his coffee cup steaming and his laptop humming to take a closer look out the big bay window.

Yep, he thought as he spotted a patch of red and gold through the lower boughs of a stand of cedars. Jeremy's trademark colors. What was the kid up to? No way would Amanda let him wander around; Colt just couldn't see that. She was a protective mom. Which meant the kid had sneaked out on his own.

That couldn't be good. And why was the boy messing around with the mailbox?

Questions that needed answers. Colt grabbed his coat, found his boots in the foyer. The first breath of winter morning air was like inhaling dry ice. Every boot step along the snowy walk and down the driveway echoed like gunfire. "Jeremy?"

Nothing. No sign of red and gold anywhere.

Colt kept trudging. In the luminous snow around him, he noticed deer prints trailing toward the lake. Bird tracks on the top rung of the rail fencing. And little boy boot marks marching right up to the mailbox, then circling back and leading off into the thick stand of cedars at the edge of his property.

"Jeremy?"

The mailbox flag was standing at attention. What was up with that? Feeling watched, he yanked open the lid. Inside was a single envelope. "To Santa" was written in cherry-red crayon.

A low branch among the stand of trees shivered, shedding snow.

"Jeremy, I don't know how to get this to Santa Claus. Maybe you should leave this at the town post office."

A face peered out between the evergreens. "Aren't ya gonna read it?"

"What for?" Kids. Who knew how they thought? Wait, maybe this was starting to make sense. "You saw me slip that money in the donation can. Is that it? Do you think I could afford to buy you some toys?"

"No!" The kid raced into sight, snow and branches flying in his wake. "You gotta read the letter! I don't want *toys*."

"I don't get this. What is this about? This is addressed to Santa Claus."

"I know about your secret identity! I haven't told no one. Honest! You gotta read the letter."

"All right, let's head in and I'll call your mom. Then I'll take you home. You can explain on the way there."

"*No!* You can't. Mom *can't* know."

"We have to tell your mom."

"But it's a secret. If I tell, then the wish won't come true. You *gotta* read the letter. *Please.*" Tears stood in the boy's eyes.

What could be so important? Colton thought about Jeremy's sick little sister at home, and the strain that had to put on his family, and didn't know what else to do. "Okay, buddy. I'll take a look."

"I wrote it real good an' everything!" Jeremy watched, face scrunched in worry, hands fisted, as if everything in his world rested on what was inside the envelope.

Colt lifted the flap. A single sheet of grade school ruled notepaper was folded in a perfect square. So much care in those folds. So much hope and anticipation on the boy's face.

He shook open the paper and studied the words neatly printed in crayon, Jeremy's Christmas letter.

Dear Santa,
I don't want no toyz. Here's what I want. Can you make Jessie well? An fix Mom's sad heart?
　I ben good.
　Jeremy.

Jeremy fidgeted, his hands clasped as if in prayer, silently pleading up at him with all his might.

Okay, the letter wasn't what he'd been expecting. Not by a long shot. And it was killing him. Colt knelt so he was eye level with the boy. "You think I can afford to make your sister well? Is that what you're asking?"

"You can fly around the entire world in one night. That's like a miracle. I know your elves are busy packing your sleigh, but my mom is awful sad and my sister is awful sick. They need a miracle awful bad."

"Do you think I'm Santa Claus or something?"

"I know it's a secret. But you said you had reindeer so you can fly."

"That wasn't what I meant. I'm just a man. That's it. I'm not Santa." He hated saying the words that brought more tears to the boy's eyes. Remembering Amanda's words from last night, *we all need heroes in our lives,* had him taking the boy by the shoulder, bridging the distance between them. He said the only thing he could. "Maybe you'd better worry about what's real."

"You mean Jesus?"

"Why don't you try asking Him for these things? In prayer."

"But I done that. And Jessie's gettin' sicker. Mom was cryin' last night."

"All you can do is ask, buddy. The rest isn't up to us. We just have to trust Him, and do the best we can from there. That's not easy, is it?" The heartbreak on the boy's face was destroying him. "Tell you what. You come up to the house with me. We'll give your mom a call to let her know where you are, and then we'll pray for these things together. Is that a deal?"

Two watery tears hung on Jeremy's cheeks. He hung his head and nodded.

What I would give to be able to make this list come true, Colt thought, because he was getting pretty fond of Jeremy. He hadn't met a nicer boy. "C'mon, buddy. I got blueberry muffins from the bakery. You like those?"

A single nod. The boy's chin was still bowed, staring hard at the scuffed toes of his boots. He gave a watery sigh as the first flakes began to fall, airy as spun sugar, as pure as grace.

The man and boy headed to the house side by side.

Amanda left Trusty Rusty parked in front of Colt's garage doors and climbed the front walkway. The snow was midcalf deep; apparently Colt hadn't found time to shovel his walk. Two pairs of tracks marred the path to the grand front door. One pair of boots was man-size; the other was her son's.

When she'd stepped out of the shower to Vi banging on the door, panic had shot through her like semiautomatic gunfire. She'd thought something was wrong with Jessie and, wrapped in a towel, dripping water all over the bathroom floor, she'd wrenched open the door. Colt had called to say that Jeremy was at his house and that he'd drive him back in a bit.

The adrenaline had worn off in a rush, leaving anger in its place. Anger that fueled her as she trudged up to the front door. She lifted her frost-nipped hand to the lighted bell on the side panel, when she saw them through the window. Colt and her son, side by side on a big leather sectional, heads bent, hands clasped in prayer.

Anger slid right out of her like the snow against her coat. Jeremy knew better than to run off like this. He'd snuck out of the house when he was supposed to be getting dressed for church. She wanted to stay furious with him, but he looked so little, just a little boy, her little boy, his head bowed so solemnly, his hands clasped so tightly his knuckles were white. His hair was mussed, a cowlick stuck straight up from the crown of his head. He had a sweatshirt pulled on over his flannel superhero pj's. She melted, and the last tendrils of anger and adrenaline faded away, leaving her exhausted. Of body, of heart, of spirit.

She waited until the prayer was over. Jeremy's head was the first to bop up. She knocked her knuckles against the windowpane. When Jeremy's gaze darted toward the sound, his eyes rounded with an "uh-oh" look.

Uh-oh was right. She avoided Colt's gaze and stepped out of his sight. The memory of last night streaked into her thoughts. How he'd curled a strand of hair behind her ear, an intimate, caring thing to do. He was a big mountain of a man, who made her want in the sweetest of ways.

Danger, she reminded herself and forced down that wish. Willed away those memories from last night. The door swung open and there was Jeremy, with dried tear tracks on his cheeks. She crumpled inside. "Are you all right?"

"Yeah, Mom." Jeremy rolled his eyes as she pulled him into a hug.

Tough again now that whatever had been troubling him was soothed over because of the man hanging back in the foyer. Dressed casually in a wash-worn pair of jeans, a black V-neck T-shirt, and gray athletic socks on his feet, he didn't look like a man who could pay cash for this house. Although, she knew he could. If she imagined him in a suit and tie, she supposed that he'd outclass this lovely home, without a doubt.

She released hold of her son. "We'll talk about you running off later. When we get home."

"But then we gotta go to church."

"Then when we get back from church. There's no getting out of this, young man." She smoothed down his cowlick.

"Aw, Mom." Whatever sadness had caused those tears was gone. What had driven him here? she wondered. Whatever it was, she was grateful to Colt for fixing it.

It was sure hard to keep from *really* liking that man. She straightened, hardly aware of the cold blowing at her back or the snow slipping down her hat and behind her coat collar as Colt approached. Her tongue stumbled over itself trying to find the right words. "I'm sorry he bothered you."

"Not a problem."

She took one look at Colt, really saw him, the amused grin curving the corners of his hard mouth, the humor brightening his eyes and softening the lean angles of his handsome face. He towered over her, looking like a magazine ad.

And she looked like… Oh, no. Her hand flew to her head. "I'm a mess. I didn't even dry my hair. I *think* I combed it."

Stop babbling, Amanda.

"You look fine. Come in before your hair freezes. It's looking crisp."

"Oh, probably." Was she really talking about her hair? Apparently. It was easier to do that than to speak of the truth that was rising like the sun between the patches of snow clouds. Her feet seized control and forced her forward into the foyer. The door shut behind her, thanks to Jeremy.

The silence grew louder with every step that Colt took closer. She didn't know if it was the longing in her heart or the fear that he wasn't feeling this for her, too, that scared her more. Quick, she had to find something to say. Anything to break the silence. To restore a normal equilibrium. "This is a beautiful house."

"Thanks."

She didn't think she'd ever been in such a luxurious place. That was probably imported marble beneath her feet, from some faraway country she'd only read about in books. It certainly looked as if he was doing very well in life. "What is it that you do for a living?"

"I'm in the computer industry."

Well, that explained it, but she had a little girl waiting for her at home, a son who needed a serious sit-down talk, and more things on her to-do list than she could possibly do. She should not be wondering about Colt. Thinking about his life. Wondering if this was one-sided and she was alone in her feelings, or if he felt this secretly, too.

It didn't matter. There were too many reasons why there could never be more than friendship between them. This house was proof of that. Their modest cabin would fit in the space of that living room and the dining room, which she could see through elegant French doors.

Best to get back to her life. "C'mon, kiddo, let's let Colt get back to his peaceful morning."

"But what about the muffins?"

Colt stalked closer. "Yeah, what about the muffins?"

"Muffins?" She felt as vulnerable as a wild bunny in front of a towering bear. She wasn't in mortal danger; no, it was only her heart. She was going to start wishing for the impossible any moment.

Leave, Amanda, before it's too late.

Unfortunately, her feet stayed glued in place.

"I promised Jeremy access to the blueberry muffins stash." Colt held out his hand, his palm wide and capable looking, a silent invitation. "A promise is a promise."

Too late. Her hand found its way to his. They were palm to palm, and her soul sighed. He felt so solid and steady, so *close,* she no longer felt so utterly alone. "I—I've got to get b-back to Jessie."

"Then we'll pack the muffins to go."

Amanda realized her hand was still resting on Colt's and pulled away. Alone, again.

"You look like a woman who hasn't had her first cup of coffee. Follow me."

"Is it that obvious? I guess I was staring a little. You're right. I need something hot to wake me all the way up." Better he believe that than the real reason. She watched her son trot off at Colt's side, staring up at Colt as if he'd transformed into a superhero.

Yeah, she knew just how her son felt.

"Sugar, milk or coffee creamer?" Colt asked from a black marble countertop in a kitchen that looked as if it belonged in an interior design magazine. "I've got hazelnut or chocolate raspberry. Wait, you want the chocolate one, don't you?"

Before she could answer, he pulled a bottle from the stainless steel refrigerator and slid it onto the counter in her direction.

"Wow!" Jeremy stared at the family room off the back of the kitchen. "Cool TV. It's bigger'n me!"

"Don't touch it, Wonder Boy." Amanda caught him by the shoulder before he could smear that expensive-looking screen. She leaned to whisper in his ear. "Maybe it'd be best if you didn't touch anything."

"Not even the blueberry muffins?"

"Smarty." She ruffled his hair and they smiled together.

Colton filled a tall, insulated travel cup with steaming coffee from the brew station and a mug for himself. He set both on the counter, watching mother and son. For the first time since he'd walked into this house, it no longer felt empty. For the first time in more years than he could remember, he didn't feel empty. Without purpose. Alone.

He dug the carton of muffins out of the pantry, so fresh the scent radiated through the plastic box. He watched Jeremy's eyes widen followed by another "wow." What he felt was wow, too, but not for the baked goods.

Jeremy climbed onto the swivel chair at the breakfast bar and knelt on the cushion, twisting the chair back and forth. "Those are the biggest muffins ever!"

Amanda shook her head. "Sit. You know better than that."

"These are the funnest chairs ever!"

"Fabulous. Sit on them the correct way." Amanda settled into the chair beside him. "He's apparently really excited to be here. Why are you here? You might as well tell me now."

Colt slid a spoon across the counter and placed the tall cup in front of her.

"Bless you," she said, upending the creamer into the steaming brew.

Yeah, she looked as if she'd had a rough night. This close up, before she'd taken the time to put on the finishing touches, like doing her hair, he could see the strain on her sweetheart face. Her porcelain complexion was nearly translucent with exhaustion, making the circles beneath her eyes as dark as bruises.

He wanted to protect her. To take care of her. To make her life easier. His spirit steeled with a resolve, something he'd never felt before. He wanted to ease the worry from her face and the sadness from her heart. He snapped open a grocery sack and slid the box of muffins inside. "There's enough for Jessie and Vi, too."

Her eyes shone with appreciation over the rim of the coffee cup. She inhaled her first sip and smiled.

Faith was a funny thing. He'd filled his life with so much work and responsibility and ambitious goals for success that his faith had gotten shoved to the side. Not forgotten, but it had become convenient. Going to church had become something he had time to do only on the major holidays every year. Christmas, Easter. He'd always figured there would be more time for attending church later in his life. Except there never had been. He'd simply become more wrapped up in his business, in being even more successful and too busy to sort out the reason why his life wasn't working. Why he was growing more and more unhappy.

God had been nudging him along this path for some time now. Colton could see that clearly. Sometimes a man had to run himself out before he was ready to appreciate a slower, better path. A more purposeful life.

He poured a cup of chocolate milk for Jeremy and handed it to him. "Do you want to tell your Mom, or should I?"

"No, you can do it." Jeremy grinned up at him. "She won't get as mad at you."

"Sounds like a fair deal to me." He leaned back against the counter, crossed his arms over his chest and studied her. Her hair drying every which way, mussed by her hat and tangled by the wind. Her pink sweatshirt and worn jeans were nothing fancy, but lovely on her. She looked like home, like happiness, like hope on Christmas Eve. He liked that. A lot. "Jeremy somehow got the idea that I have a secret identity."

"No, he didn't." She arched one brow, staring at him through the steam from her cup. "A secret identity? Who, exactly did he think you were?"

"Someone jolly."

"Who flies with reindeer. Santa Claus. Of course. Tell me he didn't give you a list of the toys he wants for Christmas?"

"He didn't."

"That's a relief."

"He wanted his little sister to get well."

Amanda lowered her cup to the counter before she dropped it. There were a lot of things she and Jeremy needed to discuss when they got home, but his heart was in the right place. She so loved him for that, her good little boy. And at the same time, his request was a knife to her heart, a reminder of what she stood to lose.

Don't look ahead. Just think about this moment.

"We have to go." She scrambled to her feet. Vi was taking good care of Jessie, but Amanda needed to leave, as much for Jessie's sake as for her own. She needed to be away from Colt. "Thanks for the coffee."

"No, take it with you."

"But the cup—"

"I'll be at church. You can give it to me then."

Amanda clutched the cup, determined to keep her

true emotions from showing. *Please, God, help me here.* Her feelings for Colt were absolutely way too strong.

Somehow, she managed to get her and Jeremy to the door. She had her cup, she had her coat, she had her car keys. She could see Trusty Rusty parked out front. She ushered her son out into the snow, falling faster now, the wind feeling more cruel.

"Thank you, for being so good to him." She feared her entire heart showed in those words.

Colt shrugged one wide shoulder easily, as if to say no big deal.

But it was a big deal to her. "If I don't make it to church, Vi will take Jeremy for me."

"Why aren't you coming? Was it something I said?"

"No. It's just that Jessie wasn't feeling well, and I might decide to stay home with her instead. I'll make sure Vi gets this back to you."

"The cup's not important. Your daughter is."

She bit her bottom lip, as if to keep whatever she was about to say from spilling out. She pivoted on her worn hiking boots, stomped down the pathway after her son until she was more shadow than substance in the falling snow.

Colt heard Jeremy's voice sounding far-off. "Yeah, I'm really sorry, Mom. But Colt 'n me, we already fixed it. We prayed for Jessie to be well in time for Christmas. We asked Jesus to help her."

A car door shut, a startling sound in the hush of the winter storm. Colt watched the headlights snap on and the car head down the driveway. He watched until the red glow of taillights faded into shadow.

He was finally ready to give name to what he was feeling. To what was happening to him. He was falling for her, for gentle, caring, captivating Amanda.

The problem was, he didn't know if he was ready for this. Or, more importantly, if she felt this for him. She had a very ill child, a child that she feared would soon need to be hospitalized. Who might not make it to Christmas.

Any hopes for a future had to be impossible. He prayed on it at church, where Amanda had not come. He prayed on it late at night, when another storm battered the house like hopelessness.

No answer came with the dawn. Just another day of wind and snow and bitter cold.

Chapter Seven

Amanda. Colt halted in midstride, his hand out-stretched to push open the bookstore's door. The nip of the bitter wind and the strike of the icy snow vanished as he drank in her welcome sight.

Her hair was drawn back into a tousled, last-minute ponytail, but the escaped strands curling down around her lovely face only made her look more dear. Her head was slightly bent over the new comic book, the gentle G-rated story of the latest adventures of Wonder Boy. She closed the softbound book and added it to the small stack she carried.

As if she could sense him standing there, she turned toward him, not surprised when their gazes met. Locked. A spear of sorrow sliced through him; it was her pain he felt. The fragments of her sorrow and broken hopes cutting deep.

He went to her. It wasn't a conscious decision. It wasn't even something he was aware of. Suddenly he was beside her and he'd folded her against his chest. She clung to him, her free hand curled tight in the fabric of his shirt, leaning against him tentatively, as if she were uncertain, as if she expected him to take a step back and leave her standing alone.

No way, lady. He tightened his hold on her, splaying a claiming hand at her nape. He could feel the graceful column of her neck, the bump of vertebrae against his palm. So fragile a woman, so Herculean her heart.

Tenderness blinded him. He breathed in the wholesome, vanilla scent of her shampoo and treasured the silken feel of her hair against the bottom of his chin. Yeah, he was falling for her—hard and fast. There was no stopping it.

"I'm sorry." She pulled away.

It killed him to let her go. He wanted to protect her. He wanted to take away every drop of her pain. Overwhelming love struck like the leading edge of a full-scale blizzard, but when he would reach to draw her close again, she took a deliberate, almost frightened step away.

"I'm sorry." She set her chin, determined. "I just had my feet knocked out from under me. I shouldn't have—"

"No, it's okay," he told her, cutting her off before she said the words he couldn't stand to hear—that she didn't care for him, that she didn't want him. "I noticed you weren't in church yesterday. Jessie?"

Agony twisted her face. Answer enough.

Sorrow left him weak-kneed. "You were waiting on test results."

She nodded, wrenching away. "Sh-she's declining very rapidly."

"She could go back into remission again, couldn't she?" He waited but she didn't answer. "There's a chance, right?"

"Anything's possible." But in her heart, she knew the answer. Amanda fought to hold on. She would not break down. She would not give in. She had to be strong—for her children's sake. "That's why I'm here. We're having Christmas early this year. So that Jessie has one more Christmas at home, in case—" She cleared the emotion from her throat. "In c-case she d-doesn't—"

She couldn't say the words. She refused to think the words. The possibility was too catastrophic to contemplate. Christmas might come too late for Jessie this year.

"Is that why you're here? Buying presents?" he asked.

"For our celebration tonight. She has to go into the h-hospital tomorrow. The doctor said to take this last day and make it count."

"Then let me help you to do that."

Her rigid self-control broke at the weight of his hand on her back. The soothing connection, the solid feel of his strength made tears burn in her throat. Tears she would not let fall. One day left, that's all she had to give her daughter before hospital beds, doctor's visits, painful IVs and scary procedures. Isolation and progressing illness and no comfort anywhere. "I don't see what you can do, Colt."

"I can be here for you."

Like a friend, of course, that's how he had to mean that. But her heart shamefully wished for more. Needed more. "Do you want to come tonight? Jeremy would love to have you."

"Even if I'm not a superhero?"

How did she admit that she thought him super enough?

He leaned closer still, so that they were nearly nose to nose, breathing the same air. "How about you? Do you want me there?"

Better stay away from that with a ten-foot pole. It was safer, less revealing, less vulnerable to stick to the facts, Amanda thought, as she moved a step back. "Turkey dinner's at six-thirty."

"Can I bring anything?"

"Just bring yourself."

"No. I *will* help you. End of discussion."

"But—"

"You should be home with your daughter, not running errands."

The next thing she knew, he was holding the books that had been in her hand, and the lump of emotion that had been searing her throat was now blurring her vision.

"Great. And I have your list, too." He rocked back on his heels, looking pleased with himself, radiating a strong essence of strength and uprightness. The kind of man who stayed when the going got rough.

To her, he was too good to be true. She couldn't find the right words to tell him so; she could only gaze up at him and pray that her heart didn't show. That she could find her way to the door and walk away from this man, so kind and dependable, who made her want to dream when she was all out of dreams.

Her footsteps sounded hollow as she headed to the door. "I have an account at most of the stores here in town. Just have them add those things to my tab. Maybe I should speak to—"

"I can handle it." He cut her off, speaking so calmly and in command that she could see him running a company. She could see why he'd been so successful in life.

Yes, I can handle it, too, she told herself, her hand sliding to her mother's cross. She would be strong enough. And if she wasn't, then she would wing it. She would somehow get through, doing her best for her kids. For Jessie. She would give her a loving, wonderful Christmas before it was too late.

The bell above the door chimed merrily, strangely at odds with the bitter, heartless snow falling. Always, endlessly falling.

Amanda looked up from draining the potatoes at the sink, an odd awareness shivering through her. A few moments later distant headlights hovered in the darkness far down her driveway, growing closer until it became a big black truck lumbering to a halt in the meager reach of the carport's lights.

Realizing all the water was gone from the pot and there was nothing pouring out but steam, she set the potatoes on a nearby trivet. Her attention remained on the man silhouetted in the faint glow of dash lights. She felt the brush of his gaze, of his sympathy through the darkness.

Why did he have such a hold on her heart? Even when she willed away her feelings for him, there they remained, tenacious and deep-rooted. Any affection for Colt was simply not allowed. Gratitude, yes. Friendliness, yes. Appreciation, yes.

Love? No.

"Let me add some milk and butter to those potatoes."

Vi shouldered close, searching through the drawers for the whisk. "The gravy's bubbling, the beans are cooling. That leaves the potatoes, and I can whip them, if you want to go greet our esteemed guest. It was real decent of him to come help us celebrate."

"Very."

"He called me, you know. Asked a few things about gifts for the kids. Clothes sizes. What kinds of things they liked. And a few other things."

"What other things? He had my list. Everything we needed to have for tonight was on it."

"I suppose he has his reasons. I've never met anyone like him. He's been a real help to us, hasn't he? Jeremy's heart has been less burdened, since you told me about their talk. It'll be a shame when Colt heads back to California. Do you figure he'll stay through the holidays?"

"No. I suppose he has his brother and friends to celebrate with."

"I suppose you're right." Vi sighed, measuring milk from the gallon jug. She'd given up on her well-intended suggestions about Amanda needing a good man in her life.

They both knew she didn't need romance; there was nothing she wanted more than for Jessie to live and see another Christmas. No, to see eighty more Christmases. *That's* what she wanted, Amanda thought, and she'd trade anything, give up any happiness for herself for that to happen.

Although she'd already tried that bargain with God, too, to no avail.

Wiping her hands on a dish towel, she glanced over the counter separating the rooms, aching for the sight of her daughter. Jessie was wrapped in her favorite pink blanket, in her warmest flannel pj's, although the woodstove kept the house toasty. She hugged Brittany Bunny with both hands, motionless in Uncle Ed's arms. Her dear button face was so pale, she looked bruised.

My poor baby. Seeing her like this was simply another blade to her heart. Amanda tore her eyes away, willing down every sorrow. This was not the time for tears but for treasuring every moment she had with her child. Still, no matter how hard she tried, sorrow choked her.

Needing something to do until she could get her emotions back under control, she headed toward the kitchen door and hauled her coat from the rack. The freezing storm pummeled her, and she let it, glad to feel something other than sadness. Snow scoured her as she hurried down the freshly shoveled walkway.

Colt slammed his back cab door, balancing an enormous cardboard box in his arms. "What are you doing out here?"

"Coming to help you."

"Some help you're gonna be if you freeze. You've got no hat, no mittens."

"Neither do you."

"Yeah, but I'm tough. How about carrying the ice cream and pie? They're in grocery sacks on the front passenger side." He popped the door open. "I didn't know there was such a thing as peppermint ice cream."

"You apparently don't know what's important in life. Peppermint ice cream with chocolate sundae syrup is one of the best desserts in life. I thought a classy guy like you would know that."

"Ice cream is one area where I'm lacking. I'm a workaholic. That leaves little spare time for dessert."

"No dessert? That simply can't be a good way to live." She swept the bags from the floor mats, taking care to hold the bag with several pies in it level. "You know, we only need one pie."

"They had a sale." He shut the door and walked to keep her in his wind shadow. "I don't know much about pies, either. I'm apparently lacking a lot."

"Restraint, too? What is in that box? That's a lot more than what was on my list. What did you do, go buy out the toy store?"

"Pretty much. You said you wanted to make this a good Christmas for Jessie, right?"

"Sure, but—"

"Merry Christmas." He leaned close and closer still until they were eye to eye, nearly mouth to mouth.

Was he trying to kiss her? Startled by the idea, she took a step back.

He stared down at her with his dark eyes unreadable, silhouetted by the porch light behind them. He pushed open the door. "After you."

Oh, so he'd been reaching for the doorknob, that was all, she thought as she stumbled through the doorway. He hadn't been harboring romantic thoughts toward her. How embarrassing. Maybe it was because, under different circumstances in a different place in her life, she would fall in love with him to the very bottom of her soul.

She held the door, leaning on it a little for support, feeling her spirit stir as he shouldered into the kitchen.

Jeremy bounded into sight. "Colt! Colt! You came! You came!"

"Sure I did. Look what I've got. You want to help me put this under the tree?"

"You know who else brought presents on Christmas Eve Night?" Jeremy leaped toward the living room. "The Wise Men! We got the story on TV right now."

Colt lumbered through the kitchen, excusing himself to Vi, who was holding the bowl of steaming homemade dinner rolls and had to wait for him to pass. "Goodness, is that all for the kids?"

Amanda nodded, unable to speak. As she shut the door, she could see Jessie perk up, her blue eyes sparkling with wonder as Colt knelt down before her, letting her peer into the box. The big man and little girl spoke, their words lost in the background noise.

Oh, how her heart ached with the sweetness. Amanda shrugged off her coat, snow sluicing to the floor mat.

Vi returned from setting the rolls on the table. "What a blessing. This is just what we all needed. This might be a last-minute celebration, but the spirit of the holiday, the goodness in men's hearts, is reassuring, isn't it?"

Amanda's throat tightened and she couldn't speak.

"Oh, what do you have there?" Vi took the plastic grocery sacks. "How many pies does that man think we need? Well, better too much than too little. Oh, there's a chocolate cream. Bless him."

He did seem heaven-sent.

Amanda made a place for the ice-cream cartons in the freezer, sending sidelong glances toward the living room. Ed had taken Jessie onto the floor, where she watched, her hands clenched with excitement, as Jeremy and Colt took the gifts from the box and spread them beneath the colorful, festive tree. Over them all, the treetop angel cast her light like a blessing, a shining hope, from above.

For one perfect moment, it was as if there was no such thing as cancer. As if such a horrible thing could never exist. Just the merry voices of children oohing and aahing over the beautifully wrapped presents topped by foil ribbons and bows. The flash of tree lights and the glint and gleam of ornaments.

For one perfect moment, it was a joy-filled Christmas Eve, like any other, like so many they'd had in the past.

Vi announced dinner was ready as she carried the platter of sliced turkey to the table. Amanda hurried to grab the last of the serving bowls, wishing she knew how to hold on to this perfect moment of grace.

And to make it last.

It was like looking at the past and the present side by side, like the picture in a picture feature on his television. Colt stuffed in the last bite of pie, already way too full from the delicious meal, and let the tastes of chocolate and whipped cream and cookie crust remind him of Christmases past.

Of his mom, when she was alive, hurrying around the apartment, after she'd rushed home from work, filling the kitchen with the scents of good things to eat. More important were the family traditions of ham and gravy, mashed potatoes and green beans—his brother *had* to have green beans—and chocolate pie.

Sadness hurt like a broken rib, all the family he'd lost—his dad, then his mom, and the traditions that went with them. Last Christmas he'd spent alone at his Malibu property with his computer humming and his work spread out in front of him. He hadn't minded it…at least, that's what he'd told himself.

Jeremy had said something to make everyone laugh; Colt had missed what it was, lost in thought. But he didn't miss the flash of merriment that reflected in the faces of the people surrounding him at this table. Ed's grandfatherly kindness and wry humor making a comment that sent Vi and Amanda into a laughter fit. Something about a Christmas disaster years ago, when Amanda's mother had been alive.

He'd never seen her like this, bright with laughter, beaming with happiness. She was luminous. Relaxed. Cradling her daughter in her lap, one hand pressed gently, soothingly against the curve of Jessie's downy head, holding her close. She pressed a kiss to her child's soft hair, clearly treasuring this time with her.

She doesn't deserve this. Jessie doesn't deserve this. No one does. Emotion—a tangle of frustration, injustice and grief—jackhammered against his sternum. Never had he felt so helpless. Or so moved by the tides of his heart.

The sudden scrape of a wood chair against linoleum rang above the clang of flatware and the conversation. Jeremy hopped to his feet. "Is it time for the presents now?"

He'd hardly been able to sit still through the meal. Maybe he'd gone a little overboard in the toy department, Colt thought as he laid the fork on the empty dessert plate. But the truth was, he had two more equal-sized boxes in his living room, ready as a surprise for Christmas morning. The pleasure of thinking about how happy the kids were going to be changed him, too.

"Please, please, *please?*" Jeremy hopped in place, bursting with excitement. *"Pleeeease!"*

Ed burst out laughing, Vi chuckled softly and pure love shone in Amanda's eyes. "Goodness, don't bust a seam, Wonder Boy. I suppose we could do presents now."

"Yaaaaaay!" Jeremy bounced around the table, shouting all the way, as hyper as if he'd inhaled a pound sack of sugar. He hopped in place as if his feet were springs, waiting for everyone else to catch up with him.

"Gotta put a new disk in the camera first." Ed shoved away from the table and rummaged around in the kitchen.

"They're in my purse, Ed," Vi called as she rose to help him.

From his chair in the corner, Colt had a perfect view into the shadowed kitchen. The long-married couple took a private moment at the far end of the kitchen, side by side, searching through their things. Ed's arm went around his wife and he whispered something in her ear. Pure love shone on Vi's face, apparent even in the darkness.

Now that's what I want. The wish came from the deepest places within him. It was providential, wasn't it, that he'd never felt this soul-deep longing before, until he met Amanda. She cradled her daughter as she rose from the table, her gaze finding his over the top of Jessie's red-gold curls. Happiness glinted through the tears in her eyes, joy shining up through the sadness.

He followed her into the living room with the flash and glow of the Christmas tree. Jeremy had dropped to his knees, looking but not touching, vibrating with anticipation.

"I've got the first present all picked out," he said the moment Colt crouched down next to him. "It's *that* one. It's for Jessie."

"It's good that she gets the first one," Colt agreed. "Here comes Ed and Vi. Wait until he gets his camcorder in place, okay? I bet he wants to give your mom some really good movies of tonight."

"It's takin' *forever.*" Jeremy was trying so hard to restrain himself.

The instant Ed had settled into the recliner and said, "Film rolling," the boy leaped into action. He grabbed the gift for his sister and flew across to the couch where she snuggled cozily in her mom's lap.

Pure delight shone on Jessie's button face. The store-wrapped package glittered with pink foil ribbon and a matching bow. "Pretty." She hugged it close, for it was a soft package that held a fuzzy pair of foot pajamas. The salesclerk had promised it would make the wearer feel like a little bunny.

Jeremy started handing out more presents. One for Vi. One for Ed. Two more for Jessie. He started a stack for himself. Jessie was giggling with happiness as she ripped open the package and discovered the fuzzy pajamas inside, pink and lavender to match Brittany Bunny.

Jeremy hooted with happiness as he found another present with his name on it under the tree.

"Thank you, Colt," Amanda said.

Her words were lost in the chaos of the joy-filled room but not the look in her eyes or the meaning in her heart. He could read both even through the noise. It wasn't happiness only that made him feel as bright as those jewel-colored bulbs blinking hopefully on the tree.

It was more the sudden awareness of his life starting anew, as if the years to this point had just been a warm-up. Prep work. For his true purpose in life—loving her.

Chapter Eight

How did she hold on to the sweetness? To never let it go?

There was no answer to that. All Amanda could do was to hold her daughter for one moment longer, and then the next, feeling grateful for this time she'd been given. How could her heart be breaking and happy at the same moment? There was no answer to that, either.

Only Colt, quietly, capably picking up torn shreds of wrapping paper and lengths of ribbons from the floor. Filling the big box he'd brought all the presents in.

Jeremy had torn through his pile of gifts and sat head bent examining his loot exclaiming, "Wow" and "Cool" and "Mom, look!" He investigated the Wonder Boy books, official T-shirt, a baseball cap and electronic gizmos she couldn't see for the tall pile of discarded packaging surrounding him like a fort.

Things were going more slowly for Jessie. Her little hands had gotten tired from ripping so much wrapping paper, and Vi had taken over for her. With one arm tight around her new dolly, she pointed at the gift she wanted opened next.

"This is pretty big." Vi tugged the designated present from the pile on the coffee table. "Ed, are you gettin' this?"

"Just had to slip in a new disk. This works slick as can be, but you gotta wait a minute. There." He snapped the camera back together and knelt down. "Ready. This makes a nice picture, Amanda, you holding Jessie like this."

It was what he didn't say that brought tears to her eyes, tears she blinked stubbornly back. This was a way of freezing time, in a fashion, of holding on to this night forever. She pressed a kiss to the soft crown of Jessie's head, refusing to think of tomorrow or of the doctor's gentle sympathy when they'd spoken early this morning on the phone.

All that mattered was this moment. This beautiful, irreplaceable moment.

"Oh, look!" Vi ripped away the snowflake-imprinted paper to reveal a brightly colored box. "It's one of those game system things. A portable one."

Amanda leaned slightly forward to get a peek at the box, but she was distracted by Jeremy and Colt heading to the kitchen. The junk drawer opened with a rasp— they must be looking for batteries or scissors.

"I don't know if I approve of video games." Amanda took a closer look at the box. "And isn't that kind of young for her?"

"Oh, it's for preschoolers. Look." Vi ripped off the last corner of paper. "These are learning games. Oh, they look fun. And wholesome. Well, I'll be." She handed Amanda the enclosed game cartridge, a DVD that showed an animated pine tree talking to an animated maple tree.

It taught about friends. And math. How sweet. Amanda turned the game over. Nichols Industries was the manufacturer. Why did that ring a bell? She'd heard of that company.

"And look, it plays movies, too. It's portable, just right for…" Vi didn't finish.

The hospital. When Amanda looked at the gifts Colt had chosen on his own, they were all things to bring a sick child a little solace. Books and fuzzy pajamas and games. As Vi opened a few of the smaller presents, wholesome children's movies and Bible stories began to make quite a stack on the coffee table.

"Isn't that thoughtful of Colt?" Vi shone with admiration as she glanced toward the kitchen.

Amanda could make him out, head bent, scissors in hand, Jeremy at his side. Thoughtful? Yes. Perfect? Yes. Did she adore him even more?

Absolutely yes.

Something troubled her, but it was just beyond her grasp. Something familiar—

"You know—" Vi leaned closer and dropped her voice "—he owns this com—"

"Mom! Mom! Look! Wonder Boy action figures. I can help a lot of people with these." Jeremy hurtled into the room, holding up Wonder Boy and his sidekick in each hand and flew around the couch with them. They circled over Jessie, making her laugh.

"It's past someone's bedtime," Amanda commented.

"Not me! Wonder Boy doesn't have a bedtime." Jeremy bounded into the dark and around the other side of the kitchen.

Colt leaned one muscled shoulder against the archway between the rooms, amusement shaping his smile.

"See what you've done?" Amanda asked.

"How is he ever gonna wind down?" Colt's gaze followed Jeremy making another revolution through the living room. "He's gaining speed. Soon he'll be supersonic."

Jessie clapped her hands, watching her brother make another loop. Amanda didn't mind much that Jeremy wasn't supposed to run in the house; Jessie's laughter was rare these days.

"Outta disk space," Ed commented from the recliner. "Jeremy, come help me haul your loot to your room. Amanda, this is a gift from Vi and me. We know yours got lost in the move."

"Ed, you and Vi—" There were no words. It shouldn't take the harder times to appreciate the wonderful people in your life, but these days she treasured and respected her aunt and uncle even more. "Thank you."

"You just push this doohickey here, and you can watch everything on the disk." He set the new camcorder on the table. "I'll detain Wonder Boy there and get him wound down for bedtime. Deal?"

"Deal." Amanda held on tight to the little girl in her arms. "It's past your bedtime, too, baby."

"A story, Mommy." Jessie pulled at a new picture book in the unwrapped pile.

"You got it, cutie." She took the book and, holding her child close, slipped from the room.

Colt watched her go, sticking to the shadows in the kitchen, feeling whole—truly complete—for the first time in his life. As if finally all the jagged pieces of his lifetime fit. Amanda may have dodged his attempt to kiss her outside in the snow, but he thought he'd seen the wish on her face—the wish for more between them.

Ed ambled into the kitchen and opened the refrigerator. "I've come for a piece of pie. Want one?"

"Why not?" He watched Ed pull out what remained of the chocolate cream pie. Colt nodded and took two dessert plates from the upper cabinets.

Ed set the foil pie plate on the counter. "You seem fine enough, for a rich guy from California. Jeremy sure seems fond of you."

Okay, where was this going? Colt had the feeling Ed hadn't come in for just a piece of pie. He hauled forks out of the drawer. "He's a great kid."

"He surely is. Me and Vi, we're pretty fond of him and Jessie and his mom."

"I can see why." Colt waited while the older man sliced the chunk of pie that remained in half and dumped one on each plate. It was hard not to like Ed; his father had been a lot like him. "You're wondering what I'm doing hanging around here."

"Sure I am. I promised my dear sister, Amanda's mom, before she passed, that I'd watch over her. Now, Amanda's having a hard time of things with her little one so sick and likely to get worse. No one wants that, but it's just the facts. So Amanda doesn't need anyone hurting her. One man's already let her down, and her heart's burdened enough."

"I'm not about to hurt her. Believe me. That's the last thing I'm here to do."

"Then why are you here? Don't get me wrong—that was a real nice thing you did for the kids tonight, but I gotta ask. Vi told me you wanted the name of the private investigator we're using. What are your intentions?"

"The best kind." Colt met the man's steely gaze.

"All right, then. I'm gonna hit the nightly news."

"Maybe I will, too." He took his plate and followed Ed into the living room. He chose the overstuffed chair instead of the couch because he could see Amanda across the length of two rooms, snuggled next to her daughter in bed. The bedside table lamp cast a soft white glow over mother and child.

She was like a vision, one he'd never tire of admiring. He watched her tense slightly, as if she were aware of his gaze. She didn't look up.

So she wasn't going to acknowledge what was building between them. Fine, but he wasn't through with her yet. Not by a long shot. She could run, she could procrastinate, but she couldn't halt the progression of this relationship.

Their first kiss was going to happen. It was just a matter of when.

In the hushed shadows of the bedroom, Vi tucked Brittany Bunny safely beneath the covers before kneeling down at Amanda's side. "Your baby is sleeping. Let me take the first shift."

"I can't leave her." This could be Jessie's last night at home. Amanda couldn't stop the panic rising up like a monster in the dark. Time was moving on, she hadn't been able to stop it—of course. "I'll just sit here for a while longer."

"Nonsense. You go check on your son and that man out there waiting for you. Then you get some shut-eye if you can manage it. Tomorrow is going to be a long difficult day, and this little girl is gonna need a mom who's rested enough to be there for her."

"You're right. You're always right. I just don't want to take my eyes off her."

"I know. But I'll be here. You'll be one room away."

There was no one she trusted more with her kids. That didn't make it any simpler to leave. It felt as if she'd ripped out her heart and left it behind as she tore herself from the room.

Colt hadn't left yet. He was at the back door, she could see him from her position in the hallway, helping Ed carry the serving dishes that Vi had brought and various other things to the car. The back door closed behind the two men, and they were out of sight. She whispered a quick thanksgiving for the reprieve. She knew Colt was waiting to talk with her, alone. Just the two of them.

Somehow she had to keep her feelings at bay, keep her regard for him secret. Easy, right? In theory, sure, when he wasn't in the same room with her. But all through the evening as they'd been opening presents, he'd been everywhere she looked, in the background, but she'd consciously noticed him there. She cared for him more than she wanted to admit.

Overwhelmed, she paused in the middle of the living room, which was in awesome disarray, a few missed scraps of paper, forgotten glittering bits of ribbon and tinsel and unwrapped toys. Colt had made this wonderful celebration extra special, with his generosity and his thoughtfulness. While Christmas was not about presents and bows, not at its heart, he had made Jessie's Christmas Eve an example in kindness.

He'd made her children happy, and if he was to walk through that door right now, how was she going to be able to hold back the wealth of love in her heart for him, for what he'd done tonight and for the man he was?

Impossible.

The back door opened, and there was Colt in all his six-foot-plus grandeur. Wait, it was the man's character that made him so huge in her view. His heart that touched hers despite everything. Too bad she had no more dreams left for herself.

"Colt." His name passed across her lips before she could stop them or alter the sound of admiration in her voice.

Good going, Amanda. He'll never guess that you like him now—not. She rolled her eyes. So, he just might be on to her.

Her hand shook as she reached to open the dishwasher. "Is Ed gone home?"

"He asked me to tell you goodbye. He'll be back in the morning early." Colt remained in his snow-dappled winter gear. "Is your little girl settled and asleep? Is she okay?"

"She's finally out like a light. You know, don't you,

how much what you did means to us?" Her hand shook again as she opened the dishwasher.

"I didn't do so much. Ran a few errands. Bought a few gifts. Normal holiday stuff."

"The things you got Jessie, they were thoughtful. They were meant to make her hospital stay a little better. You know the doctor said if her condition keeps deteriorating like this, if she continues to decline at this rate and she isn't responding to their treatments, then—"

Agony left her shattered and she quickly snatched a plate from the counter and scraped it over the garbage disposal. Focus, Amanda. Keep it together. "So what you've done for her is…I don't know the word. I'll be grateful to you for the rest of my life."

Blindly she stabbed the plate toward the dishwasher rack and slipped it into place more by feel than by sight, the way she was doing everything these days. "I know you are simply being a good neighbor, a Good Samaritan, a man acting on his faith tonight, with your generosity and goodwill, but it has mattered so much—"

You will always be a hero to me. She bit her bottom lip to keep the words inside her heart. A secret best kept. She reached for another plate without seeing it, scraping, slipping it into the dishwasher. Another. Blocking the sound of his footsteps coming closer, a soft pad of boots against the linoleum, approaching slow and deliberate. Her pulse skyrocketed when he halted behind her, so close she could feel the air between them.

His hands came to rest on her shoulders, fingers

splayed and radiating comfort and a connection that chased away the shadows of loneliness within her.

He leaned so close, she could detect the subtle masculine scents of winter wind and snow and woodsy aftershave and feel the heat of his breath against her ear. "Let me take some of this from you."

She shivered all the way to the bottom of her soul. "You want to do the dishes? But you're a guest, and there's no way I'm going to let you—"

"I'm not a guest. That's not how I see things at all." His fingers dug into her shoulder with careful firmness, not to bruise but to direct her back away from the counter. "You look like a woman who needs to put her feet up and have a hot cup of tea."

"I can't do that." Couldn't he see all that she had to do, and all of it weighing like a two-hundred-pound barbell on her shoulders? "There's so much to get done for our early Christmas morning, and Vi's asked our pastor to come and I need to make sure to take enough sausage and bacon from the freezer to thaw for our big traditional breakfast, and—"

"Shh." He brushed his lips to the side of her cheek.

That *wasn't* a kiss, Amanda, she told herself. It was just an accidental touch, since they were so close and he was walking her to the table.

She dug in her heels, stopping their progress. "I have to sort through the clean clothes in the laundry room I haven't folded yet, and get things ready for Jessie. I have to pack. I have to get her favorite books, make a list…that's what I need to do, so I don't forget what's important to her—"

"Fine. You can make a list right now." With deft pressure, he got her moving forward again. "You drink some tea and make a list. I'll do the rest."

"No, this is beyond the call of a good neighbor, Colt. And I'm uncomfortable with pity and I don't want to be your charitable cause. Don't get me wrong, what you've done for us is just short of a miracle come true, because I've been so alone—"

Stop Amanda, now, before you spill your entire heart. How humiliating would that be? Very.

She snuffled in a breath past the sorrow balling up in her throat like tears. "You need to go home now. It's late, and it's not proper for you to be here."

"That's a good excuse to get rid of me, but it's not going to work." He bumped her forward a few more steps and tugged out the closest chair with his foot. "Sit. Rest. Let me help."

"But, I—"

"This isn't charity and it isn't pity and it isn't good works." He spoke with authority befitting a successful businessman.

Her knees weakened and she found herself in the chair.

He gave a half smile as he pulled a second chair for her to put her feet on. She was too awestruck to protest. Too awestruck to do much of anything but watch as he poured a cup of tea from the kettle simmering on the warmer and served it with honey and the pen and notepad she kept by the phone.

"Write," he instructed and went to tackle the dishes.

Her vision was blurry again. She blinked hard, holding down her feelings. Staying in control. The angel hovering on the treetop blurred into a soft iridescent glow.

She felt for her mother's cross, taking comfort in the warm familiar gold and the symbolism behind it. Over two thousand years ago when the world was so dark and cold, a child had been born. A Savior, who gave His life for mankind so that everyone who believed in Him, adult or child, large or small, through all time would have eternal life. A saving light in the hopeless dark.

"You're crying." Colt's calming baritone against her ear. The pads of his thumbs rubbing away the damp on her cheeks.

She hadn't been aware of his approach. Or of him kneeling before her. She was aware of him now.

"What can I do for you?" he asked. "Anything. Just name it."

"If you do one more thing for me, you're going to win my heart for eternity."

He paused, no emotion showed on his face. "Maybe you should open your present, Amanda."

"My what?"

"I wanted to give it to you when we were alone." He produced a small gift and set it on the table in front of her. "We're alone."

Were they. Although Vi was one room away, it was hard to be aware of anyone or anything, not even the store-wrapped present faintly reflecting the pulse of the tree lights. All Amanda could see and feel was the heart of this man, stalwart and kind.

Remember, you can't keep falling in love with him,

Amanda. He is not yours to keep. "You're being too nice again."

"I told you, I'm not nice. I'm a dedicated, workaholic businessman. Ruthless."

"You're not ruthless."

"Okay, that's true. But let's just say you and your kids have inspired me to be better. A better man. A better Christian. Better at everything." He laid his hand against the curve of her face, gazing into her eyes as if he could see her soul.

You're reading too much into this, Amanda. She felt her soul stir, her spirit lighten, her heart fill with hope she had no right to.

"Open it." He didn't remove his hand or break the bond of their gaze. "Please."

Her fingers tugged at the bow, and it gave her something to do, something to look at and think about other than the man kneeling before her. The gold foil ribbon became a golden smear as her eyes began to smart.

No more tears, Amanda. But she couldn't seem to stop them. Couldn't stanch the flow of emotion rising through the shadows and the fear, until suddenly the paper had fallen away and a small, hand-carved jewel box stared up at her.

On the lid, inlaid in opal, was the silhouette of a mother and a small daughter, kneeling toward one another, heads bowed together, hands clasped in prayer.

"I saw it and thought of you," he said.

"It's p-perfect." The only words she could manage before the first tear fell. The only tear she would allow to fall. There was no stopping the turn of the world spinning on its axis, no stopping the seconds slipping past like water through her fingers.

"I have been praying for a miracle for so long now, I'm numb from clasping my hands. Hoarse from uttering the same plea over and over. The thing about God is that He might not answer my prayers at all, but every time I'm out of strength, out of hope, out of mercy, goodness comes into my life. Ed and Vi offer me their vacation house and a job in their shop. The community church starts a fund drive for Jessie's medical bills. And now you, as if you were heaven-sent."

"Hardly heaven-sent. How do you do it? This is what amazes me about you. Your daughter is terminally ill and you are unwavering in your belief. Most people would be angry with God for allowing a nice little girl to suffer like this, maybe turn their backs on Him. But you…I'm awed by you."

She was cracking apart, her shell brittle as an uncooked egg, and his words, his regard tapped at the cracks. Mortal blows. "You have no idea. I'm drowning, going down for the third time. And my faith? It's not un-wavering." She studied the tree angel casting her gracious light. "It's just that I have nothing else left."

His touch never wavered. "What do you mean?"

"I've run out of faith long ago. I feel as if I'm just groping my way through an endless dark. Lost. But I have to keep believing. It's all I have. Because that's my child in there, the heart of my heart. And if there is no miracle, if she runs out of time on this earth and no prayer will keep her here, then the only way I can let her go is trusting in His promise. I have to believe that she will be carried in the arms of an angel to heaven and she won't be alone."

Colt felt bleakness wash through her and into him. And her only hope, her stark truth of faith, paralyzed him. A supernova of certainty blazed to life within him. Certainty and too many layers of love to name brightened until he felt overshadowed.

"I have to go sit with my little one." Amanda rose, darting away from his comfort. "Thank you, Colt. For everything."

And she was gone, leaving him in the light-shadows of the Christmas tree blinking from the other room. He knelt in a shadowed dark, but for the first time he could see clearly.

The faint hint of moonlight struggled pale and opalescent through the closed miniblinds. He didn't know what compelled him to go to the window to witness the black mantle of clouds beginning to rip apart, snow still tumbling from the heavens. A small slice of moonlight dared to glow on the backs of the falling flakes and the darkly stretching reaches of the snow-covered forest.

It felt silent and sacred, and Colton could almost see the brush of angels' wings in the breaking storm.

Chapter Nine

Heaven felt so far away.

Amanda watched her daughter sleep, feeling claws sinking deep into her heart. Claws of hopelessness and powerlessness. She could not stop the night from slipping away, second by second, minute by minute. Hour by hour.

Help me to handle this, Lord. She was shredded on the inside, a slow steady bleed of pain that was gaining momentum. Soon it would be powerful enough to wash her away like a flash flood. Her daughter needed hope, and Amanda was all out of it. Her daughter needed belief, and all Amanda had was the dog-eared Bible in her lap, full of wisdom and promises and reassurance she could not feel through the agony.

For my child's sake, please guide me. I'm not strong enough to do this alone.

No answer. Heaven was definitely too far away.

Vi padded into the room, a steaming mug of tea in

hand. "I left yours in the kitchen. Take a break. Get something to eat. It'll be dawn soon, and the kids will be up."

And there were more presents to put under the tree before then. Wordlessly, Amanda rose to her feet. She backed toward the door, watching as Vi settled into the bedside chair to keep watch. At the threshold, Amanda paused. The next step would take Jessie from sight and it felt like ripping her heart out.

Please help, angels. She waited, gathering strength but no strength came. She'd been up all night, and the exhaustion of it settled on her mortal being like an impossible weight.

No help came.

Jessie slept, as relaxed as a rag doll in her new bunny pajamas. One arm was wrapped around Brittany Bunny, the other around her new doll. How sweet. Amanda had spent most of the night memorizing her daughter's dearness, her red-gold curls, her button nose, her cherub's face, trying to record in her memory the way Jessie gave a hum now and then in her dreams.

Amanda filled with equal part unconditional love, equal part suffocating grief. She felt that today, moving her into a hospital bed, would be the first step toward losing her. *We're almost out of time, Lord. Out of time for a miracle and for hope. I'm running out of time to be with her. Please, stop the dawn from coming.*

Another impossible prayer, she knew, but it didn't stop her from asking just the same. She was so over her limit, so out of everything. She choked down a sob, refusing to let it escape. She *would* hold it together. She *would*. Somehow. For her children's sake.

She wrenched away from the doorway and went in search of the promised tea. Sure enough, there it was, steaming on the table next to the small jewel box Colt had given her.

Colt. His words came back to her, and the sincere note in his baritone seemed burned into her soul. *Your daughter is terminally ill and you are unwavering in your belief.* What was on the surface hid the struggle inside. Even this morning when it did not seem as if her prayers could possibly be heard, she was still holding her Bible with both hands, needing the tangible proof of a promise she could no longer feel.

Colt. She stumbled to her feet, feeling his nearness even before she saw the sudden flash of headlights lumbering around the corner of her driveway. A tiny light of hope sparked to life within her. He'd left last night after cleaning the kitchen and, sensibly, she thought that was the last she'd see of him.

All night long, a foolish part of her wished he'd be here with the sunrise.

No wishing allowed, Amanda. If she had to wish, she would save it for her daughter. Besides, Colt was a neighbor and a friend—nothing more. He'd given her no reason to think otherwise. She had to be realistic, even when her heart ached with wonder at the sight of him climbing out of his cab in the inky darkness.

He was barely visible against his black truck, shadow upon shadow, but she sensed him moving closer as if her spirit turned toward his, like the stars faced the north pole, bound by a force she would not name. She would *not* give name to the affection rising through her like dawn. It would be easier to ignore that way. Easier to control, push back down and deny.

Colt. There he was at the door. She could see him through the window over the sink. As if he felt her presence, his gaze found hers with pinpoint accuracy. Her love for him brightened a notch.

She fumbled with the door without realizing she'd crossed the room, letting Colt in with the cold. The first thing she saw was the huge box he carried in both arms. Unbelievable.

"Surprise," his baritone rumbled tenderly.

That had to be her imagination, right? The box he carried looked full of presents; a faint gleam of an edge of a ribbon and the curve of a bow confirmed it. He ambled through the half dark toward the tree, lights out, angel shadowed.

"I think Jeremy was right." She shut the door and trailed after him, whispering. "You have to be a super-hero. Don't tell me you deliver presents around the world, too."

"This is my first stop." He lowered the box to the living room floor. "I thought I'd see how it goes here, and if it's successful, I'll branch out. What can I say? Jeremy inspired me."

"You do look a lot like Wonder Boy in this light."

"Wow. Too bad my cape's at the dry cleaner."

They both managed a smile at the line that had started all this between them. Then she backed away, just a step, but created distance just the same.

Colt battled down the urge to reach across the distance she'd created and draw her into his arms. To hold her safe and show her how he meant for things to be from now on. That he would shoulder the burdens that drew sadness into her lovely face. That he was her rock, her support, no matter what, for the rest of his days.

Before he could move closer, she knelt to study the contents of one of the boxes, moving away, but only delaying the inevitable.

"I told you that you've done more than enough already, right?" Affection—he was sure that's what it was—brightened her soft alto.

His love for her intensified and he was eclipsed by the power of it. Pure and brilliant and perfect, and it shone through him as he knelt, the box between them. How did he begin to put his enduring love for her into words? Any word would be inadequate.

"You know what I said, right? That if you do one more thing for us, you're going to win my respect for eternity."

"That's not how I remember it." He withdrew the envelope from his coat pocket. "You said that I'd win your heart."

You already have. And all the layers from top to bottom. She ducked her chin, shielding her face from him. *Amanda, you cannot fall any further in love with this man.*

It was not the material things he'd brought them. What captivated her, what made her adore him beyond the reaches of her heart, was his goodness. It shone through him like the stars through the galaxy. Every second that passed, every minute that ticked by, she loved him more.

Amanda, you have to stop this, right now. But it was like ripping out a part of her as she climbed to her feet and retreated to the kitchen. She was already danger-ously perched on the edge, and any kind word from him, a touch, a smile, a look, that's all it would take to topple her right off into lifelong, honest devotion to this man. This was so not what she needed right now.

Think about your daughter, she commanded. Don't wonder what it would be like if he miraculously loved you back. That would be impossible.

Do something, do anything. She grabbed the notepad with her packing list. Maybe she could get started, quietly, on a few of these things, without waking up the kids. As for Colt—

He'd lifted the flap of the envelope and pulled out a sheet of paper. "This is an e-mail from one of the top P.I. firms in the Southwest. I hired them to help Ed's friend find Jessie's father. It says here they've picked up his trail in El Paso and they're hopeful. And this—" he pulled out a check "—this is for Jessie."

Amanda stared at the check. It was made out to her and signed, but the amount was left blank. That couldn't be right. No one writes a blank check.

Some cog in her brain stopped working and she couldn't make her thoughts move forward. She couldn't think. She couldn't breathe. She couldn't blink.

This could not be real. It simply couldn't be.

"You fill in the amount. Whatever that is ought to cover everything she needs." He pressed the check into her grasp.

The to-do list she carried, flat against the cover of her Bible, was now mostly covered by a check. *A blank check.* The cog stuck in her brain didn't move.

Her heart did, plummeting to the soles of her feet.

He'd given her money. Money for Jessie. But, but, but, she thought, her mind still stuck in place. *But* a charity hospital would probably cover the costs of a transplant. *But* there had to be a donor who matched first. *But* this meant Jessie had a fighting chance.

The check blurred into a smear of black ink. Her heart was still grounded. This is hope, her mind told her. This is a sign. Maybe this is a turning point. Maybe Todd can be found. Maybe he's a match. Maybe Jessie will recover and have eighty more Christmases, each happier than the last. Hallelujah.

But her heart remained defeated. How on earth can that be? Nothing mattered more than her children. So why did the check feel like another difficult loss?

She recognized the name on the check. Colton Nichols. Nichols Industries. Colt wasn't just a successful businessman who lived five driveways down. He was a millionaire a hundred times over. If she paid more attention to the local gossip and probably to news in general, she would have known it was him, right off.

But her world had been reduced to providing for her children and caring for ill little Jessie. She wasn't even sure what the day's date was, only that today she had to pack her child's things for a long hospital stay. Maybe her last hospital stay. Or, maybe the money would make no difference in the end. *Oh, I do hope it will,* she prayed.

But, irrationally, it was as if all the starlight had died in the sky. As if the promise of dawn would never come. And that made no sense at all. She heard the sob rip from her throat but it felt disembodied, as if from someone else far away, someone in terrible agony.

His warm hands cupped her chin, cradled her face. Big, engulfing, capable hands that made the deepest part of her spirit brighten, impossibly, with a love she could not allow.

His eyes glowed dark, locking on hers, probing deep as if he needed to see into her very soul. "This may not be able to save your child. I know that. But this way, you don't have to worry. Not about insurance paying or not paying. Not about co-pays or deductibles. Not about finding Todd. If you do, then not worrying about the logistics of getting Jessie's transplant paid for."

I can't take anymore, she thought. Another sob tore up from the deepest places within her. She couldn't take any more kindness, any more glimpses of hope, any more threats of despair. What she couldn't do was to stop the love she felt for this man—this faithful, bighearted man—from flaming to life like a new star burning until it eclipsed all else until there was only an endless, soul-deep devotion and admiration for him.

This is only charity. *Only*—and yet it was everything. A chance for Jessie. A partly answered prayer.

Not love.

Well, she thought as she struggled to hold on to her heartbreak and her hope in the same breath. She'd known that all along, right? All that mattered was Jessie. It's all that mattered, from the top to the bottom of her soul. So, her feelings made no sense at all.

"I'll a-always b-be—" She was crying, sobbing out the words. "G-grateful."

"This comes with no strings attached." He didn't let go of her, holding her so she could not escape.

Didn't he know that his words were another cut to

her heart? "I kn-know. You're a g-good man, C-Colton Nichols."

"Not even close. And with that said, there's something I want you to know. I'm staying. I'll run my business from here. I might have to take a few trips back to L.A., but I can do most things here. What I will not do is to let you go through this alone."

"No, I won't let you do that." Not as a friend. "You've d-done enough, and I'm p-perfectly capable of handling this—"

"Shh." He cut her off, moving infinitesimally closer. "I'm not leaving you to face this alone. Or any hardship. Not for the rest of my life."

She saw it then, the glimpse of his heart, the one she'd never seen before but it was the same blinding light that burned inside of her. How could it be? He didn't love her, did he? He'd never said anything, he'd never hinted, he'd never been anything less than a gentleman. Which, of course, she realized, he was.

He was showing her now. It was in his touch and in his voice. Blazing like forever in his eyes.

"I am so in love with you, Amanda Richards. I have to ask you a question."

She felt suspended, gazing up at him, his hands cradling her face. Her mind had gotten stuck again, her heart had taken another tumble. Her entire being stilled as she felt his question. "Y-yes," she answered.

His chuckle was pure joy. "I didn't ask you anything yet."

"I know, but I can feel it in my heart. Like dawn coming."

"Like Christmas coming early." His lips hovered over hers, drifting ever closer.

"I love you," she whispered just a millisecond before their lips met. Before his kiss sealed his unspoken promise with honest tenderness. It was a tenderness she would cherish for the rest of her life.

Like a gentle sunrise, light blurred the edges of Amanda's vision. She heard a faint rustle and the pad of stocking feet. Colt lifted his lips from hers and pulled her tight against his chest. "Look at Wonder Boy."

There was Jeremy, grinning in the gleam of the Christmas tree. The angel's pure white light drifted over them like grace.

Epilogue

Christmas Eve, two years later.

"I think he's *finally* asleep," Amanda whispered to her husband and carefully closed Jeremy's bedroom door.

"Jessie is, too."

Amanda joined Colt in the hallway, catching a glimpse of her daughter asleep in her bed. Joy brimmed every time she looked at her child. Todd had been a match, after all. The bone marrow transplant had been tough, but Jessie was a real trooper. With her illness past, she looked like any healthy little girl, snuggled in for the night.

God had been gracious, so very gracious.

The third door was the nursery. Little Annabelle Rose, named after both their mothers, smacked her lips in her sleep, a contented sound.

Amanda's heart filled with thankfulness for these wonderful blessings.

In the living room, the Christmas tree cast jewel-toned hues against the long bank of windows of their Moose Lake home. Outside, through the dark glass, it was snowing, sifting like spun sugar onto the snow-covered deck that faced the lake. A fire crackled in the stone hearth; the house was expectant and silent. Even the treetop angel seemed to be waiting.

It had been a busy two years, but heaven-sent. She'd gone to work as the head of their new charity, which helped families with critically ill children. Her life had purpose, love and happiness, and all because of the man who drew her into his arms, who had kept all his promises. He was a real man, a wonderful blessing, who had changed her life.

"Do you know the best thing about this Christmas?" she asked, gazing up at his beloved face.

"We don't have to have it early. This year, it's right on time."

"And I have a feeling that from here on out, every Christmas will be merrier than the next."

"Believe it." Colt kissed her, long and sweetly, on this holy night full of hope and grace.

* * * * *